I0638029

Joan Byrd

Also by Joan Byrd
From Indigo Sea Press

The All My Tomorrows Series:

A New Beginning

Love Finds a Way

Today, Tomorrow and Always

Keeping Watch Over You

Love Never Ends

Finding Kris Kringle

Made by the Master's Hand

The Untold Stories of Jesus

Rabach

The Box in the Attic

The Good Seed—the Bad Seed

The Devil's Revenge—God's Victory

Sunset Over Dixie

The Missing Christmas Card

The Shadow of the Moon Rider

The Seed Has Been Sown

The Battle for Heaven

The Lost Sheep

The Forbidden Forest

indigoseapress.com

Giving Hearts

By

Joan Byrd

Deep Indigo Books
Published by Indigo Sea Press
Winston-Salem

Joan Byrd

Deep Indigo Books
Indigo Sea Press
302 Ricks Drive
Winston-Salem, NC 27103

For information regarding bulk purchases of this book, digital purchase and special discounts, please contact the publisher at indigoseapress@gmail.com

Cover Design by Pan Morelli
Manufactured in the United States of America
ISBN 978-1-63066-593-7

Dedication

I dedicate *Giving Hearts* first to my loving husband Ray Byrd and his twin brother Roy Byrd. Ray and Roy were placed in the Methodist Children's Home in Winston-Salem, N.C., when they were toddlers and called it home until they left at 18 years old. Growing up in an orphanage with a lot of other orphans meant having a big family with several good friends among them. They played together, worked together, worshiped together, went to school together, and got in trouble together, then found themselves digging in the ditch on Saturday, together.

Ray and Roy Byrd

Once a year, the first Saturday in May, the home kids known as the Children's Home Alumni, return to their home campus for a day of reuniting with one another. Being married to a "home kid," I now find that I am part of this fine group of people. I have heard all of their many stories so much, I can feel like I was a part of all those adventures with them, even helping shovel out the dreaded ditch with the Byrds, the Murdochs, and the Tuttles! I can tell you truthfully, never have I met a more loving giving group of Christians.

One more reason for their great upbringing was their beloved leader, my third dedication, Pop Woosley. I believe of all of those faithful people in charge of looking after so many children, Pop Woosley would be the one I would have loved to have known. It was such a big part of each child's life, I bet if you asked them today, who at the home did you look up to the most, Pop Woosley's name would come up.

Today, under new owners, things they remembered and

looked forward to seeing again are being torn down. The lovely old houses they grew up in—gone. The once grand dining hall, torn down to be replaced with ranch style houses. The only things remaining now look sadly lonely. The old gym, the barns, and Woosley Chapel, without its beautiful pews, removed for chairs.

Pop Woosley

As night falls over the old campus an old familiar sound can be heard in the growing mist. Footsteps, making their way down the old paths, long gone, past a row of stately old homes, glowing dimly in the shadows of yesterday. The sound of many little footsteps approach, behind one invisible man, singing in his old familiar voice the song he had sung so often while he lived among the children. If we grow still and listen, we just might hear Pop Woosley singing:

> *This is my father's world:*
> *Why should my heart be sad?*
> *The Lord is king: let the heavens ring*
> *God reigns; let the earth be glad!*

—Joan Byrd

Woosley Chapel

CHAPTER 1

Asheville, North Carolina, 1955

Christmas was only one week away. The big white house at 3390 Pinebrook Drive sat ready for the holidays. The eight-foot Christmas tree stood majestically in the big arch window, brightly aglow with sparkling lights, the true colors of Christmas, red, green, white and blue. Candles stood stately on the large cypress mantel and glowed from every window in the three-store mansion called Andersen Hall.

Beautifully wrapped presents had been placed in a perfect display around the magnificent tree, but the large space in front was reserved for Santa's gifts for the Andersen's twin daughters, Ashley and Allison, who had just turned five in November.

Despite being wealthy, Cornelia enjoyed doing her own cooking, especially baking all her Christmas treats she gave to friends and family. So, the house smelled like Christmas, from the cinnamon and ginger filling the air. Although the girls were too young to help their mama with the baking, Cornelia happily gave her daughters the job of tasting each batch before bagging them up and tying a red bow around the top.

The Andersen family loved doing Christmas traditions together, like making their rounds through the neighborhood to the older residents to sing Christmas Carols or going skating on the frozen pond just on the outskirts of town. But their very favorite tradition was to unbox the old antique manger scene passed down in Cornelia's family and save the baby Jesus to place in his manger on Christmas Eve. It would remain wrapped and hidden inside the box until then.

At five years old, Christmas was a magical time for the twin girls, but on that night the unexpected happened after everyone had gone to bed. Where the fire started was never discovered and the loss was devastating, not only for the neighborhood but even more for little Ashley and Allison Andersen.

They were awakened by their father as he lifted them up, one in each arm, and ran out the house, setting them down at a safe distanced as he told them:

"My little darlings, please stay right here until daddy goes back to get your mama!" With those last words, Richard Andersen ran back inside the burning building and was never seen again.

As the firemen tried to save the once beautiful home, their brave efforts were in vain. Some neighbors nearby had brought blankets to wrap the shivering girls from the winter night as the fire chief gave his report to the town sheriff.

"Bill, what's going to happen to those darling little twins? The house was completely destroyed and the worst part, Richard and Cornelia were overcome by smoke inhalation!" Fire chief Steelman glanced at the sad little girls who held tight to each other's hands. "How do you tell little ones they will never see their mama and daddy again?"

"Perhaps, the news will come easier from a relative, Ronnie." The sheriff signed the report, then looked up to see a white station wagon pulled to a stop near the five-year-old girls and a heavy set, middle-aged woman stepped out. Bill Baxter turned to Mr. Steelman and spoke softly. "It would appear, Abigale Andersen, the children's grandmother, is their only living relative and she is living in Willow Creek Senior Care, at ninety-nine-years old. I have been told a Clara Angelica is her caregiver." The sheriff turned to watch the smiling woman walking toward the children. "From the description of the cheerful caregiver, I'd say…"

"And you would be right, Sheriff Baxter! My name is Clara Angelica and Mrs. Abigale has sent me for her grandbabies!" The bright face woman smiled, knowing she had the sheriff completely baffled as to how she could have heard his conversation. "And you gentlemen can relax, Abigale has asked me to inform these babies about their precious parents." Clara noticed both men relax, knowing the burden of telling the two small children the bad news was hers.

Clara got down in front of the girls and held out her loving arms. Without hesitation they ran into her embrace crying.

"It's alright to cry, sweet babies. Clara understands how hard it is to see everything your little life has always known go up in smoke. Clara can also see your small hearts are breaking because, even though you are but little five-year-olds, you realize you will never see your mama and daddy again, on this earth. Do you remember being told about a place call heaven?"

"Yes, Miss Clara." Ashley looked up with her big blue eyes and smiled. "We will see mama and daddy again, in heaven, won't we Clara?"

"That's right, sweet baby girl and even though you cannot see them now, they can see you, like when you do something happy!" Clara smiled and gave them a big hug. "Now that your sweet grandma is unable to keep you with her, she has made arrangements for you to live at the Angel of Mercy Orphanage in a beautiful town, just a few miles from Asheville, called Antler Knob, right off the Blue Ridge Parkway. I can guarantee you will have a white Christmas."

"Clara, since our house burned down, how can Santa find us way up on Antler Knob?" Allison's eyes were filled with questions. "Will we be orphans, like Annie?"

Allison and Ashley

"Sweet Allison, Santa Claus can find the good little girls and boys no matter where they're at. Old Saint Nicolas puts the magic in Christmas!" Clara chuckled at the girl's bright smiles. "And when you live and grow up at Angel Mercy, you might be an orphan, but you never go without a lot of love! They treat each child special and when you grow up and leave the home, one of you will decide to make Antler Knob your permanent home."

"Miss Clara, I think there's some magic in you!" Ashley

gave her a big hug, then looked sadly at her home in ashes. "Miss Clara, the fireman said everything was destroyed in the fire! We don't have any family photographs left of mama and daddy or that big family portrait that hung over the mantle!" Tears began to roll down the young cheeks as she sniffed. "How will we remember them, Clara, when we grow up? Our grandmother and grandfather Jackson died two years ago and I can barely remember what they looked like!"

"Me either, Ash!" Allison began crying as she clung to her sister and Clara. "Miss Clara, please tell us we will remember mama and daddy!"

"Sweet babies, you will always remember happy times with your mama and daddy, through one another. Their faces may fade a little but the love that you have for them in your beautiful hearts will live with you forever." Clara looked up, knowing one of the firemen had found one special thing that had not caught fire, most likely, she thought, a special gift from heaven. "Look children, the old antique manger scene!"

"Wow!" the twins said in amazement as the young fireman shook his head in disbelief.

"It's the most unusual thing I have ever witness!" He held the perfect set down for the girls to see. "It would appear everything one is here, plus the sheep, donkey, three camels and one cow, but no sign of the baby! His manger was empty."

"That's because we hadn't placed him there yet, sir." Allison gazed down at the virgin mother. "Mama kept Jesus wrapped up and kept in her room until Christmas Eve." Ashley looked hopeful. "Did you look for the baby in Mama's bedroom?"

"The fireman glanced over at Clara, knowing that's where they had found these children's parents. The entire room had gone up in flames and all that remained there were only embers and ashes. Clara could read his thoughts, so to relieve the young man from having to bring up the sad truth to the already heartbroken girls, Clara patted his back and said softly, "We must be happy with what God has spared from the flames, sweet ones and give him thanks." Clara hugged the girls and stood up smiling. "Who knows, some Christmas in your future, that sweet little baby might just be reunited with his manger!"

"You really believe that, Clara?" Ashley watched the fireman place the nativity scene in a box and place it carefully in Clara's car.

"I certainly believe in miracles and Christmas Eve is the night of miracles." Clara helped the girls in the big car, then climbed behind the wheel. "Just stay as sweet as you are and remember all the good manners your mama and daddy taught you, and I just believe that night of miracles will come true for you both!"

Clara pointed at the big white house, decorated with thousands of Christmas lights and to the girl's delight, they were shining even brighter in the falling snow.

"Here we are little babies, Angel of Mercy, your new loving home for thirteen years!" Clara smiled brightly as their shining eyes danced with total delight.

"Miss Clara, how did we get here so fast?" Allison saw her sister nod in agreement. "We only just now climbed in your car!"

"Allison is right, Miss Clara, it was like magic! As we drove away, I sadly looked back to see where our house set, and the next second we were here at this beautiful Christmas house!"

"Those little eyes just drifted off to sleep when I cut on the car's heater and you slept all the way up the mountain!" Clara winked at a cheery red headed woman who opened the door to help the girls out. "Now girls, this is Miss Mary, your housemother! I can grant you, Mary will give you lots of love, same as me!"

"Couldn't you stay with us, Clara?" Allison clung to the loving woman. "I feel safe and loved by you already!"

"Baby, I would like nothing more than to stay right here with you until you are eighteen, but my place is with your dear grandmother right now." Clara gave each girl a great big hug. "Would it make you feel better if I told you, we would meet again in the future?"

"You mean it?" Ashley laughed happily "Then you can keep our nativity safe with you until we grow up!"

"That is a splendid ideal Clara." Mary smiled as she took the girls by the hand. "We would have had to store it away until they graduate and sometimes things get misplaced with so many children."

"Then it's settled. I will deliver it to the home of Allison during the Christmas season, since she will be the one who chooses Antler knob as her home." Clara winked at the girls, got in her car and was gone in a flash.

Christmas Eve arrived and all the children raced off to the chapel for singing and receiving a gift from the staff. Santa would be bringing the younger children presents on that special night and the joy and excitement radiated from every child, except two little girls, who chose to stay behind, together, in their shared bedroom.

Ashley walked over to the only mirror that hung in the big room and looked at her reflection for a few moments before twirling around laughing.

"I'm going to be a famous movie star when I grow up and make thousands of movies and lots of money! Do you think I am pretty enough, Ali?"

"Ash, you are the most beautiful person I know!" Allison got up and walked over to hug her sister. "I bet you will be the prettiest actress in Hollywood! When I grow up, I want to be a really good mama and have lots of babies to love!" she took her sister's hand "And I will never leave my babies alone!"

"A mama?" Ashley pulled her sister to the bed and sat down, her big blue eyes sparkling with love. "Being a mama is real nice, Ali, but you could grow up to be a famous artist!" Ashley reached for one of her drawings. "Like this picture of three little kittens playing, Allison you are very good, you know!"

Allison hugged her sister and giggled "I will always keep drawing Ash, because I love to, but having children will always be my first dream."

As the twins sat in the quiet bedroom, Ashley declared "No matter what we become Allison, we will always have each other! You will come first with me and I know, I will come first with you!"

CHAPTER 2

Antler Knob, North Carolina, 1983

Bella and Clara found themselves in a small living room in a very quaint farmhouse. Looking around, the two friends saw there were no Christmas decorations up, then heard children's laughter from the next room. Peeking inside, Bella smiled at the five children surrounding their mother as she read a happy Christmas story.

"Oh, Clara, it does my heart good to see children so happy and content to hear their mother reading them a story." Bella glanced down at the big box that appeared in her friend's hand. "Clara, what have you there? Some sort of present or perhaps, a lovely decoration to brighten up the place with a little Christmas cheer?"

"It will indeed put a sparkle of Christmas in this home." Clara winked and carried the box over to the living room mantle and started placing the old nativity set out, then she stood back to admire her handy work. "Perfect! The family heirloom has return to one of its rightful owners."

"Clara, do my eyes deceive me, or is the wee one missing from his manger bed?" Bella asked innocently.

"Sweet girl, as always, your eyes are perfect! God's creations are never flawed when made in Heaven." A huge happy smile filled Clara's face. "You see, the sweet baby was never found in the ashes of the Andersen mansion, so all assumed the fire destroyed it." The angelic face lit up

"But miracles do happen, especially on the night of Christmas Eve!"

Once again, the children laughed out, so the two friends walked in, unseen by the sweet family, to listen.

"And little Jenny was not afraid anymore of the funny clown juggling milk bottles, or the school crossing guard, who blew his whistle too loud, because he was hard of hearing. Jenny had her new puppy, Jax and she would always have her guardian angel, Angelica! The end!" Allison smiled at her beautiful blonde hair, blue eyed, little darlings, then noticed ten-year-old Tyler raise his hand. "Yes son, do you have a question?"

"Mama, do we all have a guardian angel or is that just made up for the storybook?"

"Tyler, my dear boy, Angels are as real and alive as you and me!" Allison reached for him and gave him a hug. "And yes, all God's children have an angel to guard them." Her smile was radiant and filled with love. "And there are times when we need lots of angels, especially if we find ourselves face to face with a juggling clown who drinks milk or a cross guard who loves to make music from a whistle!"

The children laughed as they pictured the clown tossing bottles as he tried to take a sip or their cross guard, dancing to his musical whistle. Little Hannah wasn't laughing, she was too caught up with having an angel for her very own and not sure what they looked like.

"Mama, why can't we see our angel? Are they afraid we might laugh at them?"

"Laugh at an angel?" Allison lifted her young daughter up in her lap. "First, angels are either beautiful or handsome, because there are both men angels and women angels! We cannot see them unless they wish to be seen."

"Mama, you told me once you thought you and Aunt Ashley saw an angel." Robin, the oldest child gathered up her brothers and sister. "Remember?"

"It happened so many years ago, but there are things that happened on that night I think I shall always remember." Allison had a faraway look, as though she were trying to piece beautiful memories together.

"Please tell us mama." Taylor spoke up shyly. "Could you see the angel, mama?"

"Oh yes, darling. A very cheerful lady with a big, beautiful smile, that seemed to dance all over her face. I cannot recall her name, but she could do magical things and somehow take away the sadness we were feeling after watching everything we knew go up in smoke."

"The night grandma and grandpa Andersen died in that house fire." Robin lifted Hannah up from her mother's, tired lap. "You need to rest mama. I'll see the kids brush their teeth and say their prayers."

"Thank you, precious girl." Allison gave all her children a weak hug. "I'll just go write down what we need at the grocery store."

"Then, Reverend Lane is coming by in the morning for the grocery list?" Robin waved the children to their rooms, then whispered. "And, don't forget to have Reverend Lane pick up your medicine at the pharmacy!"

"Dalton said he would be here around ten in the morning, Robin." Allison kissed her almost grown twelve-year-old. "There's no need to worry darling girl, Dalton always keeps his word."

Joseph and Dalton

The two angelic friends had been listening, then watched as the family went to their separate rooms.

"Clara, Reverend Lane sounds like a very dependable friend." Bella smiled over at her friend.

"A caring friend indeed, and the good minister would like to be a whole lot more than just friends with Allison, but she cannot see the good thing in front of her because her health and children consume all her life."

"If he loves her Clara, why doesn't he just tell her." Bella's attention was on the frail woman as she struggled to make a cup of hot tea. "Clara, is Allison sick? She looks so pale and weak."

"Sweet girl, I'm afraid if a miracle does not accrue this Christmas season, those lovely children's lives will be changed forever." Clara eyes grew sad. "Allison needs a kidney transplant real soon or I will be taking her five babies to the

Angel of Mercy orphanage."

"What about Ashley, her twin sister? Surely, Clara, she would be a match." Bella looked hopeful.

"And that is where you come in sweet girl!" Clara took both of Bella's hands. "You need to convince Melinda Star to stop production on her latest hit to come here to Antler Knob for Christmas!"

"The Melinda Star? The famous movie actress?" Bella asked, wide-eyed.

"I believe this modern world prefers the label for all stars, men and women to be, movie actor." Clara shook her head. "To answer your question, yes Melinda Star is really Ashley Andersen, Allison's twin sister." The cheery woman gave a toothy grin as she patted Bella on the cheek. "Do you think you can convince this big movie star to come home for her twin sister?"

"Yes, I do!" Bella announced proudly "Somehow, someway, Ashley Andersen will come home to Antler Knob this year for Christmas!"

"That's good to hear, sweet girl, I like your positive attitude!" Clara chuckled. "Allison's attempts to reach her sister have failed." Clara nodded toward the frail woman holding tight to the telephone receiver "Mrs. Davis, Miss Star's secretary, never delivers Allison's messages to the busy actress. Oh, she got through again to Mrs. Davis. Just listen."

"Mrs. Davis, I'm glad I reached you before you left the studio. Did you give Melinda my message I left yesterday? She hasn't returned my call." Allison glanced up at a picture of her and Ashley when they graduated and parted their separate ways. "I must speak to her! It is very important!" when no response came from the other end, Allison continued "Just tell her Allison needs her to call at once, please."

"I will see that Miss Star gets your messages when she has a free moment. This is a busy time for her and this motion picture needs to be finished before New Year's. Where family matters are concern, they will just have to wait." Coldly said and to the point, the secretary hung up and tossed the message on top of the others, inside her desk drawer.

"Clara, what a cruel thing to say and do to that poor sick woman!" Bella had watched Allison stare for a moment before hanging up the phone, as tears fell down her sweet, beautiful face.

"That is why the Father has sent us, sweet girl, to help turn this around and open up the eyes of Ashley and Allison and let them see the love standing right in front of them before it is too late." Clara shook her head sadly. "Those poor children have already loss their daddy when he died four years ago from a childhood sickness.

"That would be Joseph Stevens, Reverend Lane's best friend. I remember, he was a fine young man, who was devoted to Allison and the children and a very good carpenter." Bella smiled "Joseph, an appropriate name for another young carpenter."

"That's right Bella, but it left these babies with only one parent. Now that Allison could die with kidney failure, those precious children could lose both parents. The outcome relies on your ability to make Ashley see the importance of walking out on that motion picture and coming to help her sister."

"Then, there is no time to waste!" Bella hugged her companion "I have no doubt you will bring some love and laughter to this family, Clara. I wonder if Allison will remember you and her family heirloom resting on the mantel."

"I'm sure in time, those beautiful memories will come drifting back." Clara wrapped her scarf around her neck and smiled broadly "I best get over to the good reverend's house to catch him in the morning." Clara winked "Tuck your wings and keep hope alive!"

CHAPTER 3

A knock came to the Steven's door and knowing Reverend Lane would be arriving at ten sharp, Robin opened the door, noticing the preacher was not alone. Dalton Lane stepped aside so Clara could step up next to him.

"Good morning, Robin. I've brought someone to meet your mama."

Clara gave the twelve-year-old a reassuring smile. "Hi Robin, my name is Clara, an old friend of the family." Clara's eyes twinkled, not letting the stern look from the young girl bother her demeanor as she added "I bet you were name after the Robin redbreast, who sings a happy song to welcome in the springtime!"

"I was conceived in the spring, so daddy said I was his little robin." The young girl never smiled as she continued. "The name stuck! You say you are a friend of the family?"

"That's right baby and I've come to help your mama. I hear she is not feeling well."

"I don't recollect mama ever mentioned anyone name Clara." Robin stood firm in the doorway, taught to never trust strangers by her father and taking on the role of family guardian since her mother got sick.

"Robin, you have nothing to fear from this dear God-fearing woman." Reverend Lane patted the girl on her head, bringing out a smile, for him. "Clara is a good friend of your Grandmother Andersen. She was her care giver and helped her right up to her death, at a ripe old age.

"Robin, dear, please don't keep our visitors standing out on that cold porch." Allison gently pulled her daughter out of the way and motioned the pair waiting on the front porch inside. "Dalton, you're right on time as usual. Is this the lady you called me about?" Clara noticed the same sweet smile as the much younger Allison at five. "Dalton tells me your name is Clara. Such a beautiful warm name. I cannot help but believe I knew a Clara once, a long time ago."

"That's right, my beautiful child, you did know a Clara—me. You were only five when I took you and your twin sister Ashley to the Angel of Mercy Orphanage."

"Clara, the very kind lady who made everything look like magic." Allison reached for her hand. "Please don't think me foolish Clara, but when my thoughts go back to that sad time, I think of you as an angel sent to take away our fear and sorrow and replace it with hope and love."

"Well, there are many people who believe I was sent to help them through whatever troubles or sickness they might be going through. Like your granny Andersen, I helped up until the good Lord took her home."

"Granny Andersen? You knew Ash and I called our grandmother granny?" Allison looked amazed at the simple dressed woman, who was anything but simple. "Did granny tell you we called her that?"

"Oh, I'm sure she must have, from all the times she talked about her beautiful talented granddaughters and had me fill out her birthday and Christmas cards to send you when you were growing up in the orphanage." Clara's eyes took in the sparsely filled wood box next to the stone fireplace. "She always recreated having to spend most of her wealth living at the Elms Retirement Home during the last twenty years of her life. It was her dream to leave you girls enough money to start your careers and put you through the college of your choice. The arts were rooted in your blood through your granny Andersen. Not only did she enjoy performing on stage, she was a very gifted painter and even had showings in New York City and Paris." Clara smiled at the painting over the mantle. "You have the same God-given talent as that precious lady you called granny."

"I regret all the years we missed out with her, but it couldn't be helped." Allison led her visitors to the family den. "Please have a seat while I go put on a pot of coffee for us."

"That is real thoughtful Allison, but I came to wait on you and not to brag, but coffee is one of my specialties." Without hesitation, the jolly woman helped the frail woman sit down, despite her soft protest. "Allison, I hear you have been sick and feeling weak and I'm sure, unless your eyesight is bad, you can see I am healthy as a racehorse and I have been told, stubborn as a mule when people won't take my sage advice."

Allison couldn't help but laugh as she relaxed on the sofa and permitted the friendly woman to place a cover over her legs.

"Clara, I'm not sure how you found out, unless…" Allison smiled over at the preacher, who had not taken his eyes off the beautiful blonde with the incredible blue eyes. "Dalton, did you tell this delightful woman about me?"

"Allison Andersen Stevens, I know you better than anyone in our small town, and since you refuse my help, except the honor of picking up your groceries and medicines, I took the liberty of asking this kind lady to assist you, any way she could. With the children, the cooking, and housework or just a kind word to help cheer you up until that sister of yours has the time to give you a call!" Dalton looked deep into her blue eyes and spoke softly. "Allison, you grow weaker every day and you need to save your energy." He gently took her hands "I hate to see you in pain and if I were a match for you, I would not hesitate to give you my kidney."

"Dalton, I have no doubt you would give me both your kidneys and lose your life for me and my children if you were ask to." Tears came into her eyes as she touched his face. "You have always been so very special to me Dalton, and if things were different…" Allison broke down in his warm embrace.

"Clara, you are right, this coffee is wonderful." Allison watched as the joyful lady pulled back the curtain to watch the children playing in the snow.

"Those little babies are going to be snow-babies pretty soon if they don't get inside to thaw out." Clara smiled broadly. "Reverend Lane, I bet you can build one beautiful fire in that fireplace."

"And he could Clara if we had enough firewood, but we are down to just a few logs and I'm saving those in case the power goes out." Allison smiled and took another sip of coffee as Robin and Dalton stared at the huge stack of firewood in the box.

"Mama, either there really is a Santa Claus and he came early or we have a secret Santa." As Robin looked from Dalton to Clara, Allison sat up to see what had her daughter and Dalton's attention.

"Now where did that wood come from? It is as dry as the old wood." Allison's attention went to Clara, who stood smiling at all the confused faces. "Clara, can you explain where that firewood came from?"

"Allison, sweet girl, I think Reverend Lane would agree with me when I say, the Lord works in mysterious ways!"

Dalton laughed joyfully as he stood up and walked over by the fireplace and started staking wood on the create.

"I certainly do agree Clara! God sends His light and love through all His servants."

Clara bolted out a hearty "AMEN! Besides, Christmas is coming and there is not one decoration up in this house, except that old beautiful nativity I took the liberty in returning to its rightful place." Clara noticed a question about to slip from Allison's lips, so she smiled over at her. "Like I said, pretty girl, God works in mysterious ways. Don't ask how? Just be thankful I remembered where I left it after twenty-five years." Clara noticed Robin had walked over to admire the old nativity set. The young girl bent in to have a closer look as Clara walked over beside her. "I see you have noticed the main person missing."

"Where is the baby in the manger, Clara?" Robin reached up to touch the empty manger, then looked over at the cheerful face next to her. "Are you saving him till Christmas Eve?"

"If I had Him I would let you place the baby Jesus in his little bed, but he disappeared the night your mama's house was destroyed by fire." Seeing the twelve-year-old grow sad, Clara looped her arm around her shoulders. "Now don't go fretting about that missing baby, child. Just be grateful the real baby chose to come to earth on that first Christmas night. That makes Christmas Eve the night of miracles and just between you and me, I believe somehow this little empty manger will cradle the little king on that night."

"Oh, Clara, that would be so magical!" Robin smiled,

finally feeling this special woman was just what her mama and all the children needed this Christmas. She reached around Clara and gave her a hug. "Thank you for coming to help mama and the children."

"You know Robin, how would you and the rest of your brothers and sisters, like to decorate your home for Christmas and bring it alive with the smells of Christmas?" Clara enjoyed watching the young girl grow excited with real holiday spirit. "A Christmas tree, candles for every window and to light the manger scene. An evergreen wreath on the front door and ginger cookies baking in the oven!"

"Clara, that would be most wonderful!" Then reality hit her and her smile turned upside down. "There is nothing left to put on a tree Clara. The storage shed outside caught fire during the summer and everything inside, including all our old lights and ornaments were destroyed."

"Then it's time for some new lights and ornaments and I just happen to have a few sets in my luggage." Clara winked at Robin. "I always have some decorations packed just in case I need to bring a little Christmas cheer to a dreary house."

Reverend Dalton Lane walked in carrying the groceries and medicine. Robin raced over to help him as she filled him in on their decorating plans.

"That sounds wonderful Robin! It's just what you need around here to get you in the Christmas spirit!" After helping put the things away, he took Allison her pill and a glass of water, then looked over toward the big picture window. "I think about an eight-foot Christmas tree in front of the big picture window! Everyone passing by can enjoy it too!"

"Dalton, please do not build up those kids hope when they come inside!" Allison, held up the empty glass for him to take. "We cannot afford a small four-foot tree, much less an eight-foot!"

Clara walked in carrying her arms full of boxes and glanced over at the serious couple. She broke the ice.

"I have lots of beautiful ornaments and lights, now all we need is for some good Christian volunteer to donate a 'big' tree to place them on!"

"Clara, I can think of that person!" Dalton stepped over beside her smiling. "I was just about to offer a big eight-foot-Spruce for the children..." He glanced down at Allison "like I have tried to do every year since Joseph passed away."

Allison couldn't resist smiling as she got up and made her way beside the handsome preacher and touched his hand.

"And we appreciate your generous offer every year Dalton, but we really cannot except such an extravagant gift, dear friend."

"Poppycock!" Clara looked from Allison to Dalton. "The way I see it, we need a tree! We will except your kind offer young man, but in return, we insist that you join us for Christmas dinner and help us decorate that very tall tree you're going after now!" Clara winked at the smiling minister as she escorted him to the door. "I hear Christmas Tree Land is having a half off sale today on their eight-foot Spruce trees! I'm pretty sure there's one with your name on it!"

"Clara, I would not doubt that for one minute!" Dalton bent over and kissed her before leaving, whistling O Christmas Tree. In his heart, the young minister knew he would be spending Christmas with the woman he had been in love with for a very long time.

CHAPTER 4

Bella peeked in on Melinda Star as she rehearsed a scene from her latest movie A Long Road Home. The director cut in.

"Melinda, doll, that was almost believable, but I think you can make it look even better."

"Almost believable? It felt perfect to me!" the starlet snapped. "We have rehearsed this stupid scene seven times Billy! You are just about to…" The actress caught sight of the woman waiting quietly in the wings. Everyone on the set looked to see what had drawn the star's attention and Bella tried to force a weak smile.

"Who is this girl and how did she get on my set?"

"I showed her the way in, Miss Star!" The words rolled coldly from the handsome man standing behind Bella. "She looked as though she were lost, so I reassured the lovely lady she was at the right place." His eyes rested on the beautiful face of Melinda Star who began smiling when she recognized her handsome friend.

"David, did we have an appointment?"

"Doctor Reynolds was kind enough to help me, Miss Star. I was sent by the advertising agency. They said you were looking for a new assistant."

"A new assistant?" Melinda turned to see the director's secretary running from her office, looking embarrassed. "Can you explain why the agency is sending me a new assistant, Miss Davis? What happen to Turner?"

"I'm terribly sorry for this confusion Miss Star. The advertising agency said they had someone coming this afternoon." The nervous secretary glanced over at the pretty young woman. "You are Bella Angelica?"

"Yes ma'am, I am Bella." Her smile was bright with a slight glow. "I know I'm a wee bit early, but I really need this job."

"Miss Davis, would you please tell me what happened to Miss Turner." The beautiful blue-eye blonde arched her eyebrow as she waited for a reply.

"To be honest Miss Star, Miss Turner said she had had enough of your demands and it appeared she could never please you so she turned in her resignation and walked out." Miss Davis looked at Bella with almost pity.

"I see!" Melinda Star laughed softly. "I suppose Tracie Turner did us both a favor by walking out. She couldn't even make a decent cup of tea." A warm smile fell on the actress' face as she walked over to Bella and put out her hand in a business shake. "Welcome aboard Bella! I am Melinda Star."

"Oh yes, I know! You are quite the actress or should I have said, actor?" Bella relaxed when she smiled. "The scene you were rehearsing was amazing! I thought you were almost believable too."

Billy laughed out loud, and Melinda could not resist laughing herself from the total innocence and honesty of this charming young woman. Everyone on the set seemed to relax with soft chuckles as Melinda reached over and patted her director's shoulder.

"Cute Billy, real cute." Melinda smiled down at Bella. "I think you and I will hit it off fine, Bella. Tell me, can you make a good cup of tea and draw a relaxing hot bath?"

"Oh yes! That will be easy enough." Bella smiled, knowing she had many gifts given to her to do many jobs well. "I can also make a great cup of cappuccino, Miss Star, if you happen to have a cappuccino machine."

"I'm sorry Bella, I don't own one of those." Melinda knew she was going to like having this outgoing woman around. "But, if things work out Bella, I will buy you one." The star heard Billy call for everyone to get back on the set, so she touched Bella's arm. "Just wait here, Bella. I'll be finished soon and we can go to my house."

"That will be fine Melinda, but aren't you forgetting someone." Bella motioned toward the handsome doctor who was checking out Melinda's schedule on the wall. The movie star nodded her gratitude for the reminder, then walked over and touched his shoulder.

"David, I almost forgot you were here, darling. You seem

so distance and quiet." Their eyes met and for a moment nothing was said. "David, did I forget my appointment again? Tracy never could keep me up with my doctor appointments."

"You, my dear, forgot our dinner date again last evening! I waited at 'our' Italian restaurant for two hours, finished the bottle of wine, tipped the understanding waitress, then went back to my lake house, alone, again!" David's voice remained cold, as he stared down at her.

"I'm terribly sorry David. We had an overshoot and it ran very late. I really feel bad I stood you up again, but we are already behind on this movie which is due out the first part of next year." Melinda took his hand and smiled beautifully. "Can I have a raincheck on dinner, David?"

"Just call me, if you are free, Miss Star! I will check and see if I am available!" David smiled politely at Bella, then turned and walked out.

Bella had felt the tension between the couple and recognized the love that had been separated, so she found herself speaking up before Melinda Star walked back to the set without trying to rescue her failing romance.

"Excuse me, Miss Star, while you rehearse, should I check your calendar and make new arrangements for that dinner date with David Reynolds? Time is too short to miss out on special times with a good friend."

"Bella, that is sweet dear, but I promise we can go over my calendar together later. Right now, I have a movie to finish, hopefully before the holidays."

Bella watched the busy woman go back on the set, knowing Melinda Star put her career above everything and everyone in her life. As the star rehearsed her lines, Bella spoke softly to herself:

"One way or the other, Ashley Andersen, I will see you can find your life outside this stuffy studio is far better and happier than any 'happy ever after' movie ever made!"

CHAPTER 5

The sound of the screen door slamming and excited voices meant the four youngest Stevens children had watched the cheery lady with the booming voice calling them inside for hot chocolate and cookies by the fire. They screeched to a halt when they reached the woman holding a tray filled with cups of hot chocolate and their sister Robin smiling beside her holding a plate of fresh baked Christmas ginger cookies.

"I think I called you inside just in time, before you all grew in one long icicle!" Clara chuckled at all the red faces and damp clothes. "Go over by the warm fireplace and get out of those snow- covered boots and coats first." Clara set down the tray and gathered four coats and four sets of boots. "Carefully, get yourself a mug of hot chocolate and your big sister will give you a nice big ginger cookie! I'm off to the mud room with these wet things, then we can discuss decorating the Christmas tree when Reverend Lane returns."

"Christmas tree?" The children voiced in unison as they took a sip of the delicious hot chocolate.

When Clara walked back inside the big den with Allison, the children stared at her in wonder until one little boy asked who she was.

"Children, this beautiful woman is Clara and she has come to help me for a while until I'm feeling better again." Allison enjoyed watching her precious children enjoying their hot chocolate and special cookie. Little five- year-old Hannah could not take her eyes off the plate of ginger cookies and started to reach for another one until Clara lifted the plate up smiling.

"Miss Hannah, you may have another cookie later, but I have made you and your family a wonderful big pot of chili and baked a luscious chocolate cake to go with that vanilla ice cream I found in the freezer." Clara winked at the big blue eye girl.

"You found ice cream in our freezer, Miss Clara?" Robin was amazed at the way things just appeared for this special person. "I never even knew we had coco in the cabinet until you started making hot chocolate."

"Like I told your mama, you precious little babies, God works in mysterious ways!" Clara smiled broadly as she said "So, tonight when you say your prayers, remember to thank Him for the things he has given you." She heard the preacher's truck drive up to the house. "Alright, I need two strong volunteers to help the good reverend haul in the eight- foot Spruce." Clara smiled when Jonathan and Tyler's hands flew up. "Great! That's make four of us!" she marched them to the door where the preacher stood posed to knock. "Save your knuckles, Dalton, we have a tree to carry inside."

As they walked out, the door seemed to magically stay open wide until they had the big tree completely through, then it closed silently by itself. After the tree had been placed by the big window, and the lights strung on by Dalton, Allison, Clara, and the two oldest children, everyone began to place ornaments on, leaving the big, beautiful angel until last. After unpacking the angel, Clara handed it to Hannah.

"Would you like to put the angel on the top and then we can all go into supper?"

"Miss Clara, I wish I could put the angel way up there, but she has wings and I don't." everyone couldn't help but laugh at her innocence. Dalton bent down and put out his strong arms for her.

"You may not have wings Hannah Stevens, but you're still an angel in my eyes." She laughed and ran into his arms, clutching the angel to her chest. "Are you ready to soar to the top, pretty girl?"

"I'm ready Dalton!" Hannah giggled as he lifted her high enough to place the angel over the top branch. "I did it!" her young eyes took in the beautiful tree with true Christmas magic. "She makes it finished!"

"And that means, it's time to eat!" Clara looked over at Allison, who had been watching how loving Dalton had been to her children, so she whispered in her ear. "Allison, I made way too much chili for our little bunch and Reverend Lane will have to eat out, since we took up his entire day."

"Dalton, Clara has made a big pot of home-made chili and the children and I would love for you to help us eat it." Allison had butterflies when he reached for her hand. "It's the least we can do after you spent your day helping us, right kids?"

"Please Dalton, stay!" Hannah took his other hand "Clara has made a big chocolate cake with ice cream!"

"How can I say no when two beautiful girls ask me so sweetly." His eyes were on the woman he loved when he added "It will be a pleasure having supper with my favorite family."

As the family sat around the table enjoying the "heavenly" food, Clara smiled at the Stevens' twins chatting about the day's activities, with their mouths full of chocolate cake.

"Now, we have a tree for Santa to put our presents under!" Ten-year-old Taylor glanced into the next room to admire the eight-foot Christmas tree sparkling with lights and ornaments. "Do you think Clara will bake enough cookies for Santa?"

"I wouldn't doubt it one bit, Taylor." Tyler took a peek over her way and caught Clara watching and smiling, so he bent down and whispered "Maybe she will fix Santa some of that great hot chocolate too. Santa must get cold in the night air delivering toys to all the good girls and boys!"

"I would really love to get a red bike this Christmas, but mama said Santa had far too many children to get presents for this year, so I ask for a small air rifle." Jonathan, eight-years-old, had been listened as well as young Hannah, who joined in on the Santa wish list.

"I really want a Chatty Cathy Doll from Santa!" her big blue eyes blinked joyfully as she smiled up at Clara. "I've been a really, really, good girl this year Clara."

"Yes, you have, Hannah as have all the Stevens children and Santa knows it and is filling up his red sleigh as we speak!" Clara chuckled at all the excited faces, then noticed the frown on Allison's beautiful face.

"Clara, we need to talk about this!" Allison never meant to sound demanding, but to promise her children the impossible was out of the question.

"There's really nothing to discuss my dear. It appears Santa has received each one of the children's letters at the North Pole and is prepared to deliver what they wish for." Clara avoided making eye contact with the children's mother as she continued and to prove her point, she would reveal those things yet not ask for. "Little Hannah not only ask for a Catty Cathy Doll, but also a coloring book, and a box of crayons, plus a special gift I'll not mention so Santa can surprise her!" Clara turned to Jonathan and smiled broadly, "A red bike, an air rifle, toy soldiers to line up and use for targets, plus a big surprise." The twins came next as Clara stood up and walked between them. "First, there will be a plate of cookies and a big cup of hot chocolate waiting for Santa, plus a bunch of fresh young carrots for the reindeer. Taylor wants her very own record player with some of the latest hits and a new pink night gown. Tyler wanted a train set, plus a ball and bat. Each twin gets a surprise gift also from the jolly old man." Clara walked over by Robin who was looking down embarrassed.

"Robin Stevens, you are just twelve years old, even though you act so much older than your tender young age. I know you slipped your letter to Santa, hoping no one would find out and make fun of you. I also know what you ask for was the most beautiful, unselfish thing anyone could have ask for."

"Tell us Clara. What did our Robin ask for?" Reverend Lane reached under the table to collect Allison's shaking hand.

"This beautiful girl asked Santa to bring her mama a miracle for complete healing and make her well." Clara took Robin's hands and lifted her up in a tight hug. "Precious girl, never forget what I told you about the missing baby in that manger."

Robin's eyes lit up with hope as she said softly "Christmas Eve is a night of miracles!"

CHAPTER 6

Bella followed Melinda Star through the studio and as they passed the secretary's desk, Bella stopped, causing the busy woman behind the desk to frown up over her black rim glasses.

"Excuse me, Miss Davis, but I believe you have some messages for Miss Star." Bella knew she had drawn the actress' attention when she turned to see why her new assistant had stopped to ask Billy's secretary about messages. The secretary smiled sheepishly, trying to figure out how this complete stranger would know about all the messages hidden in her top drawer.

"I can assure you, miss, we take care of all Miss Stars calls." Miss Davis spoke sharply.

"Miss Davis, Bella is new at the position and just needs a little time to learn the ropes." Melinda took a firm grip on Bella's hand and pulled her out on the street where a big limousine waited with a chauffeur standing by the opened door. After climbing inside, the famous actress smiled over at her new girl "Bella, little things like messages are taken care of when you become a big star. That's just one of the extra, you receive."

"But Melinda, what about personal messages? What does Miss Davis do with them?" Bella could see her job was cut out for her.

"Bella, you really have nothing to worry about. You'll get use to things around here soon enough." Melinda Star took the Chauffeur's hand and climbed out after the big car stopped in front of a massive mansion. "Now, come on in Bella. I am totally exhausted and need a good hot bath and a hot cup of English Tea, then it's off to bed."

"Clara, that was one of the best meals I have ever had!" Allison hugged the older woman. "Thank you so much, for everything. You are a real angel!"

"Yes, you could say that!" Clara chuckled as she watched

Dalton Lane slip another ginger cookie. "I think someone else likes my cooking!" she nodded with her head as she winked at the beautiful frail woman. Hearing the two women laughing, the preacher looked up and smiled.

"I see I've been caught!" Dalton picked up his glass of tea and washed down the good cookie, then started rolling up his sleeves. "Let's get these dishes before they set up."

"Young man, that is most generous and had I not kept you so busy all day, I might just have taken you up on your kind offer, but I noticed your eyes dropping off at the table when I read the children their bedtime story before they went off to bed." Clara started gathering plates and brushed Allison's hands away.

"Please Clara, let me help you with these dishes. You have been going non-stop as well today."

"Don't you go worrying about me sweetheart. Old Clara can work wonders!" Clara turned her around to face the preacher. "You can go see the good reverend gets out and on his way and…" she winked "Thank him proper before you say goodnight." Clara walked to the kitchen with her stack of dishes singing, as Dalton took Allison by the hand and walked to the front door for his goodnight kiss.

The next day, the family was busy making presents for their friends when Reverend Lane dropped by to deliver his gifts for each Stevens child as he had done every Christmas. There was only one exception this season, Dalton had also bought a special gift for Allison and intended to give it to her on Christmas Eve with the hope that she would except it with joy.

"I know I usually wait to bring your gifts closer to Christmas, but the big tree looked so empty around the bottom and Santa's presents won't arrive until late on Christmas Eve." Dalton winked at a smiling Clara, then helped Robin and the twins place his presents under the tree. "Now, that's much better!"

"It does look better Dalton, thank you, dear friend." Allison helped her youngest paint the solid white angel Clara had given her to give her best friend, Janie. "How is the Christmas Eve Concert contest going this year, Dalton? Shannon Wellington has a beautiful solo voice and ever since she joined the church, she has chosen to sing with our choir this year instead of her school of the arts group."

"That's right Allison. I have high hopes this year! We just might win first place and save the children's orphanage." Dalton helped Jonathan glue the wings on the freshly painted airplane. "Jon, Leroy is going to love this red plane." He held it up to admire. "The Red Baron! That is one really cool gift, my boy."

"Thanks Dalton!" Jonathan turned it around in his hand "Can you help me wrap it?"

"You bet, son." Dalton reached for a perfect size box and placed the precious gift inside. "Robin has been asked to join the choir this year, with your permission Allison." He smiled at the pretty twelve-year-old, who looked down blushing.

"Clara, what do you think? Choir members usually have to be sixteen to join the adult choir." Allison knew her daughter had a lovely mature voice, but she didn't want other in the church to start whispering about Reverend Lane showing favors for Allison Stevens.

"If it were up to me, I would give her my blessings" Clara lifted Robin's chin "but, I think we need to leave that decision to the little songbird herself. Robin, would you enjoy singing in the adult choir?"

"Oh yes ma'am, I would, very much!" The young girl glowed with happiness. "It would be an honor to add my voice to the winning group this year."

"With such a positive attitude, we will surely win this year." Dalton Lane had high hopes for this year's contest. With only one cash prize rewarded, for first place, it had to come this year if his church was going to save The Angel of Mercy from being demolished and replace by a shopping mall.

"Tis a shame that fine home for children got in such bad deterioration because funds stopped coming in to keep it up and running." Clara held her finger on the knot for Taylor to tie her bow. "I keep forgetting how things down here on earth can run down if not properly attended! "Clara's mind seemed to be moving, as unheard questions seem to float upward and that special glow lit up her cheerful face, when she received her answer. "Tell me Dalton, this group that wins every year, they are professionals?"

"They are mostly Broadway singers from New York City, each graduating from the North Carolina School of the Arts! The rules state you must be connected to North Carolina in some form and it does not matter whether you are professional or not to win the cash prize of $500,000.00!" Dalton chuckled when Tyler said, "Holy cha-moly! That's a lot of do-re-me!"

"Does anyone know who gives the prize money, Dalton?" Clara asked, even though she knew the good reverend had no clue it was Melinda Star, giving back to her community.

"The donor asked to be anonymous, but they have to be someone with a big bank account." Dalton checked his watch, knowing he had a church meeting and must leave soon. "The only thing the secret giver ask is that you strive to make the most of your God given talent and to help bring Christmas joy in the hearts of those who hear your message through song."

"Clara, the judge comes from outer state and has no way of knowing anyone trying out for the top prize." Allison had seen Dalton check his watch and knew he would be leaving soon. "I just believe up until now, the judge picked the professionals because they proved to be a little better than our amateur choir. But this year, we have a fighting chance."

"Clara, if we do not win this year, the town will demolish the old buildings, sell the property and all those children will have to be placed wherever they can find openings. Families will be separated according to age!" Dalton Lane stood up and put on his coat. "I know it will take a lot of faith and work to get that old building back to living conditions, but we have men and women waiting for a chance to restore Angel of Mercy! All we need is that $500,000 and we can at least make it livable and save it from the wrecking ball."

"Reverend Lane, remember what Clara says, Christmas Eve is a night of miracles!" Robin got up to walk him to the door. "I truly believe in my heart we are going to get our miracles this year, sir."

Dalton's eyes caught Clara's, then he smiled and hugged the sweet caring girl.

"I just think we might get several miracles this Christmas Eve Robin." He tightened the scarf around his neck "I'll be by in the morning around nine to pick you up for choir practice. Time is running out and the director called an extra practice at nine-thirty. Tell your mom!" with that, the preacher drove away to his meeting.

CHAPTER 7

All the family had got up early to see Robin off to her first choir practice as an adult. Clara had put a Christmas tape on and made spiced apple cider for everyone to enjoy while they waited for Reverend Lane. Robin, too nervous to sit still, got up to straighten up one of the tree ornaments, then stood back to admire it.

"I declare mama, this is the prettiest Christmas tree we have ever had!"

"I couldn't agree more darling. Dalton knows how to pick out pretty Christmas trees." Allison blushed just from saying his name and as not to show her true feelings she added "He is such a good friend."

"I would say, a very good friend, Allison. One of the kind, perfect to have around and a pleasure to be with." Clara walked up next to Robin and brushed through her hair. "Now, stop fretting, sweet girl, you will do just fine. Just open up and sing right from your heart, just like the angel you are."

With his mind still on the perfect tree, Tyler got up to see it closer. "Mama, the last time we had a real tree was five years ago, when Aunt Ashley came to help you with Hannah, after she was born."

"That's right! Has it been five years since I saw Ash?" Allison set her empty cup down and closed her eyes. "I was hoping your aunt would come this Christmas."

"Yeah! She brought us all those presents wrapped in fancy paper and bows!" Taylor smiled at Clara. "Aunt Ashley is a rich movie star with lots of money! She is really glamorous!"

"That's because Aunt Ashley wears a lot of make-up Taylor!" Robin walked over and hugged her mother. "Mama might not dress in fancy rich clothes like our movie star aunt or wear a lot of make-up and have her hair done up special, but mama is beautiful without all that! She has an enter beauty that comes from her heart."

"You're right baby. Your mama is a loving, beautiful person, and God is very proud of her giving heart."

"You're right about mama's giving heart Clara." Tyler walked over and knelt down at the woman who had raise him and his brother and sisters with total love. "Before she started feeling poorly, she would help old lady Smith, down the street with her house cleaning while we were in school and cooked entire meals for the food shelter once a week."

"Mama would fill in for Mrs. Hastens, my third-grade teacher whenever she needed to take her cripple little boy to the doctor or just stay at home with him whenever he took sick." Taylor kissed her mother on the cheek.

"Now children, I just did what any person of faith would do whenever some neighbor was in need." Allison smiled shyly over at Clara. "I'm no saint, I grant you."

"You're right there Allison." All the children frowned at the cheerful woman for obviously knocking their mama off the high platform they had just sit her on. "Brush down your feathers children and let me explain my bold statement in re-guards to your beautiful mama. The gospel truth is, there has been only one person born on this earth that was and is still perfect."

"Who Clara, you?" Innocents dripping off her sweet face, Hannah looked around at everyone as they laughed at her statement. She shrugged her little shoulders and took baby steps over to Clara, her blue eyes wide with confusion. "If it isn't you Clara, is it Dalton?"

Again, the laughter began as Allison stood up smiling and collected her small daughter in her arms. "Hannah, darling, Clara was referring to God's Son, the one whose birthday we are celebrating on Christmas Eve."

"Oh! Baby Jesus!" Hannah blew out her relief and smiled sweetly. "You are right Clara! Jesus is perfect! You can see it in His eyes in the painting mama made!" Hannah almost gushed with joy remembering Reverend Lane excepting it for the congregation and hanging it over the altar, smack in the middle, to draw ever eye to the Savior's face.

"Mama could have sold many of her beautiful paintings,

Clara, but she chose to give them to the person who admired it enough to offer a price." Robin checked the clock on the mantle. Reverend Lane would be right on time. "The life-like painting over the fireplace is my favorite!" Tears formed in Robin's young eyes. "Mama painted it right before daddy died, the whole family happy together."

"And your daddy told all of you that picture of all of us together would keep us close together, forever." Allison felt a little guilty for having another man on her mind lately, but in truth, Allison had always loved Dalton Lane and had felt he had pushed her into his best friend's arms years earlier.

"You are right, children, your mama has a very special gift and just like your daddy, she too will live forever with you in that picture." Hearing a soft sniffle, Clara looked over to find Taylor staring up at the true to life painting and walked over, draping her arm around the ten-year-old. "Baby girl, is something wrong?"

"Clara…is mama going to die like daddy?" Taylor whispered, not wanting her mama or sisters and brothers to hear. "Is she going to leave us like daddy?"

"Sweet child, we cannot be sure when the Father will call us home, but I can promise you Taylor, He will never leave you alone." Clara got down beside the young girl, a reassuring smile stretched across her face as she announced, "Christmas is a time for miracles child, and if you and the other children pray real hard, God will give you that Christmas Eve miracle."

Right on cue, Reverend Dalton Lane pulled up the drive at nine sharp to collect his newest choir member.

CHAPTER 8

Bella handed Melinda a cup of hot tea after she had settled down onto a soft white leather sofa. Silently watching her new assistant place a cashmere throw over her legs before taking her own cup of tea to a chair next to the fireplace.

"I just love a crackling fireplace." Bella closed her eyes and sniffed the air "The smoke smell is so warm and relaxing. It reminds me of older times."

"Bella Angelica, tell me you are referring to Old Salem or Williamsburg, Virginia." The actress laughed, knowing Bella couldn't be more than twenty. "The bath has relaxed me, enjoy the fire."

"How was your bath then? Alright?" Bella wrinkled her nose from the hot tea. "Is your tea alright?"

"Dear Bella, the bath was heavenly and the tea could not have been any better! A good strong cup, just like I wanted." Melinda sipped on the strong tea and smiled at the younger woman's obvious dislike of hot tea. "Tea too strong for you dear?"

"I guess I just prefer coffee, especially cappuccino, that's my specialty." Bella watched Melinda relaxing with her eyes shut, so she glanced around the room for family pictures or perhaps one of David. Bella smiled when she spotted two young girls hugged up, looking identical. Biting her lip, Bella chose her words wisely.

"Do you have any family, Melinda? You know, mother father, 'sister', brother, or perhaps, any wee ones?"

Melinda Star sat straight up, getting choked on her tea. Bella started to jump up to help her and she smiled, waving her back down.

"I will be fine Bella. You startled me with your question about...wee ones? Referring to children, correct?"

"Should I have not asked about children, Melinda? I would have no way of knowing if you had any wee ones, or sisters or brothers for that matter." Bella noticed the actress' teacup was empty, so she gathered the tea pot and poured her another cup. "I'm truly sorry if I overstepped my position but I do consider you a friend above my employer."

"And you are right Bella, you are quickly becoming my favorite friend." Melinda stirred in her cream and sugar, then took a grateful sip. "Of course, I don't have any children. A big star like me just does not have the time for a family life."

"That's a shame." Bella glanced at Melinda dressed in overalls next to David, in a straw hat. Happier times she thought as she continued "Do you have any other family?"

"My parents died when I was five." Melinda's attention fell on the photo of her and her sister Allison when they lived at Angel of Mercy and noticed that Bella had been drawn to it. "That's my twin sister Allison. Your sweetness reminds me of her."

"Does it?" Bella's smiled was radiant. "Your twin sister, how wonderful! You must be very close to her. I've heard, twins have a special bond because they have always been together from conception."

"Yes, Allison and I have always had a special closeness." Melinda arose from the sofa and picked up the picture, a sweet smile on her lips as her thoughts traveled back to happier times. "I remember all the fun times we had growing up, even though it was, for the most part, in an orphanage."

Bella placed her hand on her shoulder as she studied the pretty blue eye, blondes. "That was after your parents died."

"We were only five when our house caught on fire and daddy carried us outside in our pajamas. He told us to wait for him..." tears laced her beautiful blue eyes as she could see clearly her daddy running back inside the burning house after their mama. "Daddy loved me and Allison very much but his heart belongs to mama. He died trying to save her. We lost almost everything, except an old nativity scene, long gone. It wasn't much use though without the leading man." Melinda laughed softly "Or should I say, the leading baby?"

"You didn't lose everything Melinda, you had your sister and your sister had you, thanks to your loving father." Bella traced the girl's happy faces in the photo.

"Yes, and we made a promise that we would always be there for one another. It was our first Christmas Eve at Angel of Mercy Orphanage when we decided to stay in our room together instead of going to the chapel for the Christmas celebration. We were telling one another what our dream was and what we wanted to become when we grew up. I, of course, wanted to become a famous movie star, but Allison loved her dolls, had gave them all names and treated them like real babies. The night of the fire took all her babies and she cried herself to sleep every night for a very long time. So, Allison wanted, more than anything, to become a mother and have a lot of babies and name them after her dolls, Robin, Tyler, Taylor, Jonathan and Hannah."

"All your dreams did come true then, didn't they?" Bella could see flash backs of when the twin graduated and received a small inheritance. "Your parents and your dear grandmother left you and Allison a small inheritance after you graduated and was set to leave the orphanage, correct?"

"Yes, that's right, but how could you possibly know about that Bella?" Melinda looked mystified "I am certain no one knows about that except the lawyer that delivered it the day Allison and I were leaving Angel of Mercy to start our new lives."

"How I know is not important Melinda, but the sacrifice your sister made that day for you was very important to you."

"Then you know Allison gave me her part of the inheritance that day to start my career as an actress." Melinda walked over by the window and looked out at the moon filled night and saw a couple strolling down the lighted sidewalk dressed in shorts and T-shirts. "I miss the snow at Christmas. Antler knob was always so alive with the holiday season and plenty of snow to give us a magical white Christmas."

"Antler Knob is still covered in snow for that magical Christmas, and your sister needs to have her best friend home this year to celebrate the holidays with her." Bella walked over by the window and shook her head "No amount of Christmas lights can turn sunny California into the spirit of Christmas."

"That's true, but I have a movie to finish and my fans have waited long enough for my latest hit." Melinda walked back to the sofa, picture still clutched in her hand. "The day Allison loving gave me her part of our inheritance will be branded inside my mind forever. I had written a big producer in Hollywood and sent him a video of my acting. He had been very impressed and ask me to come out to Hollywood immediately for a small part in a star-studded movie. I was to report on the set the following Monday if I wanted the part or it would be given to another budding actress, Ann Margaret. My part of the small inheritance would pay for my air fare to California, but there wouldn't be enough for my wardrobe and for rent on an apartment."

"So, your sister, Allison gave you all of her inheritance so your dream could become a reality." Bella smiled warmly. "In return, you gave her something precious back, to make her dreams come true. A very special something."

Melinda could only stare in shock, thinking to herself, how does this young woman know so much about me and Allison, unless…"

"We will save that logic for another time, but for now, your sister has asked you to come home! Do the right thing Ashley. Give your sister this Christmas with your presence!"

Melinda wiped away her tears as she gazed down at her sister's sweet face. "I haven't seen Allison for four, no five years. Can you believe it?"

"No, Ashley Andersen, quite frankly, I cannot believe it at all!" Bella replaced the photo and gathered the actress' hands "You must go and see your sister. Don't put off important things like that. One never knows what tomorrow might bring."

"Yes, you are so right Bella." Melinda Star blew her sister a kiss then smiled at her young assistant, who stood poised for the right answer from the busy movie star. She never got the answer she waited for, instead the actress sighed. "You see Bella, I did become that big movie star and my darling sister did have her babies, five very active children!" she forced a laugh. "Allison is busy raising babies and I am busy making pictures!"

Bella shook her head flustered, as the actress started back to her bedroom, Bella right behind.

"But, Melinda, five years? The children are growing up without knowing their aunt Ashley and your sister never stopped needing you." Bella turned down the bed covers as her eyes met the woman she had been sent to and needed to convince the importance of returning to Antler Knob. "Melinda, you never stopped needing your sister Allison either, did you?"

"I will always need my sister, Bella. I promise, as soon as this movie is finished, I'm going for a visit." Melinda smiled at Bella and gave her a hug. "There's only four more scenes to shoot and Billy promised me I would get a vacation this year, or at least by sometime in January." She noticed the concern in Bella's eyes. "Now stop your worrying and go to bed. It's late and I am exhausted. We've got to get up early in the morning for a photo shoot before the camera rolls." Pushing Bella gently out the door, Melinda yawned and closed her door as she mumbled her goodnight.

Bella looked up to the heavens as she spoke softly "Only four scenes? Ashley Andersen does not have time for even one scene. Billy will do one retake after another and before you know it, Christmas Eve will be here and Allison's time will be running out!"

CHAPTER 9

Clara walked into the living room as Allison was hanging up the receiver, disappointment written on her tired face.

"It's useless Clara! I will never reach Ashley in time." The pretty mother laid her head back against the chair "I don't know what else to do. If I cannot find a kidney donor who is a perfect match, this will be my last Christmas with my children." Allison had felt hopeful ever since Clara came into their lives but it was hard for her to believe a miracle would be arriving on Christmas Eve.

Clara made her way over beside Allison and placed a loving hand on her trembling shoulder.

"Don't give up, sweet girl and never stop believing! Have you tried writing Ashley?"

"Write her? But, Clara, do you really think writing her a letter will work?" Allison looked up helplessly. "What makes you think they won't just toss it inside a waste can?"

"Trust me here girl, it will work, I truly believe this!" Clara chuckled. "Only, don't write the letter to Miss Melinda Star, the famous actress, send your letter to Miss Ashley Andersen, a beloved sister." Clara walked over to Allison's desk and took out a pen and a few sheets of stationary and laid it on the desktop. She motioned her over. "Now start writing and tell her everything."

"Everything?" Allison picked up the pen with her shaky fingers and took a deep breath. "It seems hurtful and cold to tell someone you love in a letter you may be dying, unless you get a new kidney immediately."

"I know baby, but if you want her to come you must tell her everything." Clara nodded, reassuring her. "Ashley will come!"

Bella stood watching from the door as Melinda posed for the photographer. The actress smiled over at Bella.

"Twenty more minutes, Bella. I will have a short break and we can go for a cappuccino."

"Sounds great, Miss Star." Bella had been asked by the secretary to address the famous actress more appropriate around the photographer and the movie staff, so she had applied. As she stood there somewhat bored, Bella jumped when someone touched her arm. Looking up, Bella was relieved to see a co-worker, the messenger Simon.

"Simon, what brings you here? Has Clara sent you with bad news?" Bella spoke softly, knowing Simon would be invisible to everyone else and might think her strange speaking to herself if they noticed her talking. Simon smiled broadly as he waved Allison's letter in front of Bella's face. She quickly grabbed it before someone found it floating in midair. "Simon, must you do these annoying things that could make me look…different."

"You are different, Bella." He teased, then looked out seriously at the famous actress. "Clara said Ashley was to get this letter, pronto!" Simon glanced sadly at the beautiful woman smiling for the camera, then shook his head. "They look so much alike, except this one is healthy, flushed with color. This letter is a matter of life and death." the messenger's eyes fell seriously down on Bella. "Literally, life and death! See that she reads this letter, soon!"

Bella waved the letter to draw Melinda's attention and at last the star noticed the frantic action coming from her loyal assistant. There appeared to be some sort of paper in her hand and Melinda Star wondered who had delivered it without anyone one seeing the delivery person. The guard standing watch at the entrance door looked relaxed by his post and those working in the studio did not appear distracted by a visitor and yet someone had brought something, obviously important enough for Bella to waved her over. How did they get in undetected and leave just as mysterious?

The beautiful actress stood up and gave her photographer a winning smile "Franklin darling, You, must have enough shots by now for Glamor Magazine! I simply must have a break before the shoot today. Shall we?" Melinda waved off any rebuttal and walked directly to Bella, who finally calmed down.

"Bella, what is so urgent it could not wait?" she smiled into Bella's serious eyes. "What is it?"

"It is a letter from your sister Allison." Bella placed the blue envelope in her soft hand. "It was hand delivered especially to you, Ashley Andersen. You must read it at once, please."

Ashley stared first at the letter, written in her sister's handwriting, then looked for a moment at the pretty assistant before she tore into the envelope and began reading. The actress felt tears stinging her eyes as she clutched the revealing letter in her shaky fingers.

"Oh! Lord, no! Bella, It's...it's Allison! She says she maybe dying soon! It cannot be, she was so healthy and full of life."

"That was five years ago, remember? A lot of things can happen in five years." Bella was relieved Ashley finally knew about her sister's fate.

"Allison says her kidneys are failing and without a transplant, they will shut down before the years end!" Ashley gratefully took the tissue from Bella's hand. "Why didn't she write me sooner! I'm sure to be a match."

"It's not too late, my friend but we must go to her at once!" Bella pulled the actress toward the door that past the secretary's desk. "You ask why your sister didn't tell you sooner." Bella took the letter and turned it over to the p.s. "I have called for months and Mrs. Davis kept putting me off" Bella handed the letter back. "Maybe you should ask Mrs. Davis what she did with 'all' Allison's messages to you."

As they rushed past the secretary's desk, Ashley stopped and stared down at the uncaring woman.

"Mrs. Davis, why didn't you tell me my sister has been trying to reach me for weeks?"

"Oh, you are referring to Allison Andersen? Your sister?" the nervous secretary faked a laugh. "I just assumed she was a disturbed fan or something."

My sister writes that she has been trying to reach me for months, and you kept putting her off!" Ashley's hand trembled, knowing her position as an important actress could have cost her dearest friend and sister her life. "I am waiting Mrs. Davis!

40

Please explain your rude actions!"

"Miss Star, you are a very famous actress! Your time is not always your own! You chose this demanding career and when the movies keep coming to please your loyal fans, then you must focus on your work, acting!" Mrs. Davis tried to sooth her. "Your sister's phone calls just slipped my mind with all the important things we must do."

"The important things?" Ashley almost screamed. "My sister may be dying! She needed me months ago! She needs me right now, Mrs. Davis! I may be the only one that can save her! What's more important than that?" Ashley turned and stormed toward the door, causing the anxious secretary to jump out of her seat and race after her, yelling.

"The picture! Miss Star, we must finish the picture on time!" Mrs. Davis stuck her head out the door and shivered from the cool breeze. "Miss Star!"

"You finish the picture, Mrs. Davis! That's not important to me! I'm going home to my sister, she needs me!" Ashley and Bella left the secretary standing with her mouth open, until the director pulled her back into the building and to her office.

"I'm sorry sir! I tried to stop her, but she would have no part of it!" Mrs. Davis sank down on her chair.

"Give it a rest, kiddo! We will just move the deadline up until Melinda's sister gets better." Billy winked at the young man who had filled him in on his leading lady's troubles. "And don't go fretting how This young man got into my office by you. Simon is a very, how shall I say it, angelic being, blessed with the ability to deliver messages." Billy reached over and patted the confused secretary, then put his hand out and shook Simon's. "Davis, give the staff a paid holiday and Merry Christmas!" Billy smiled up at Simon. "Are you sure you wouldn't like some eggnog?" then disappeared behind his office door.

Mrs. Davis stared wide-eyed at her boss speaking to someone invisible and shaking hands with...no one! She nervously typed the paid holiday announcement for the staff and sent it out. In a daze, the secretary stood up and put on her light jacket, then cut her lights out. Her eyes fixed on Billy's door when she heard laughter and voices. Slipping over, she cracked open the door to see her boss lifting a glass of eggnog in a toast, as she thought,

"Poor thing. He sure can use a holiday." Just as she was about to close the door, she heard another voice say "cheers." Peeking around the door, she saw a glass of eggnog floating in the air and grabbing her chest, Mrs. Davis let out a gasp.

"Care to join me and Simon in an eggnog, my dear?" Billy relaxed back in his seat, never realizing he was the only one who could see Simon.

"No...no, thank you, sir. You and...a...Simon enjoy your drinks! The staff thanks you for their gift, as do I. Merry Christmas!" she glanced over at the empty glass drifting down on Billy's desk "And, Merry Christmas to you, Simon."

"Thank you, Gail!" Simon smiled at her big eyes, staring at the empty space. "Christmas Greetings to you!" With that, Gail Davis raced out of Billy's office, down the hall, and out of the building, believing she had just witnessed the Spirit of Christmas present.

CHAPTER 10

Bella and Ashley rushed down the street where David
Reynolds stood waiting beside a taxicab. He opened the door
and held out his hand.

"Let's get you to the airport! Our plane leaves in one hour."

"Our plane? David? How did you know about Allison?"
Ashley asked while staring at the taxicab. "I cannot just leave
for the airport with no clothes! I must go pack first!"

"It all taken care of Ashley! I have packed everything you
might need and ask David to stop by your house on his way
here to collect them." Bella pushed her toward David so he
could help her in the cab. "By the way, I took the liberty of
inviting David, your 'dear' friend, to come with us. As I recall,
he has helped you in the past! A true friend!"

"Yes, Bella, a very good friend! Alright David, you might
be of some assistance in my sister's transplant. You are not just
a very good friend, you are one terrific doctor!" Ashley reached
over and took his hand as David slipped his arm around her
shoulders, protectively.

Ashley did not wait for introductions as she flew passed
Clara, who was standing in the doorway. Bella hugged her dear
friend and introduced David before they followed behind the
cheery woman to the den where the sisters were, wrapped in
each other's arms.

"Oh, Allison, dear sweet Allison!" tears streamed down
Ashley's face, seeing her twin so pale and thin. "I'm sorry it
took me so long to get here! Had I known earlier…"

"It's alright now, Ashley, you're here and that's what
matters." Allison suddenly felt relaxed and at peace with
herself. "If something is going to happen to me Ashley, I
believe we must tell the children the truth."

"The truth? Don't they know how sick you are?" Ashley
pulled her sister down on the sofa and took her hands. "Do you

want me to tell them you need a kidney transplant?"

"The children are well informed about my health conditions Ashley and have even been tested to see if they were a match." Allison knew any one of her precious children was willing to give her a kidney, but the test revealed it negative. All five had their father's blood type, and so did Reverend Lane, who had prayed to be the perfect match.

"Surely, I will be a match, right David?" Ashley looked hopeful over at her dear friend.

"We shall find out soon enough, Ashley. I recall the clinic hours are from eight in the morning until six in the evening, correct?" David joined the sisters on the sofa and checked Allison's brow for any fever. It was somewhat warm but no reason for alarm.

"That's right Doctor Reynolds, eight till six." Clara smiled from the doorway "I'll make an appointment and we can all go see how the results turn out."

"Thank you, Clara, that is a great ideal." Allison spoke softly to her sister. "I was referring to telling the children about their birth, Ashley. They will need you if I don't make it and the truth will draw them closer to you."

Clara walked over to the sofa and smiled down at the serious faces. "There is plenty of time to tell the children what they need to know, but for now, those five little darlings are waiting in the living room ready to show off their Christmas tree to their Aunt Ashley, along with her friends, David, and Bella." Clara beamed with total joy. "The big Spruce Dalton Lane got looks bright and beautiful in my old ornaments and lights."

"Dalton? Is he here?" David helped the two sisters up and followed behind them. "I haven't seen him in six years."

"I guess you're right David, it has been almost six years." Clara didn't give him time to ask how she could possibly know Reverend Lane's roll in the fertilization of Allison's eggs, since it had been done in secret. "You can catch up with the good reverend tomorrow at the clinic. He will be there at five p.m. when we are waiting the results."

"You've already made the appointment?" David looked

totally confused. "Did Bella call you and tell you we were flying out?"

"Something like that." Clara mused for a moment then smiled. "The children are waiting!" Clara opened the door where the Christmas tree was alive with colorful lights and sparkling ornaments. As if by demand, the children stopped what they were doing, some playing card games, others putting a Christmas puzzle together, and looked at the door. Then with excitement, raced over to greet their movie star aunt, all but little Hannah. She could not remember Ashley because she had just been born. So, Hannah hung back, behind the tree, where she could peek around at the woman who resembled her mother.

"Aunt Ashley!" came the cries of delight from the four oldest children as they filled her arms with hugs.

"We are so glad you came this year, Aunt Ashley." Robin spoke softly as her eyes feasted on her beautiful rich blue suit. "Mama really needs you."

"We need you too, Aunt Ashley!" Taylor looked around her and beyond the big door. "Did you leave our presents in the den?"

"Taylor? We cannot expect Aunt Ashley to bring us a gift when she visits!" Robin had noticed Ashley's forlorn look and realized she hadn't thought about getting presents on such a short notice. "Having you here is all the present we need, Ashley."

"It's always great having her here, Robin, but you must admit she gives terrific gifts!" Tyler joined sides with his twin sister.

"Kids, don't worry your aunt about not having you presents this year. The fact that she stopped filming right near the end of the movie, to come home, is a beautiful gift to me." Allison took her hand and noticed her sister had perked up.

"The reason why I have not got the gifts with me this year is simple! I had to leave for home before I could send Bella shopping, but now, I can personally shop for your presents right here in Antler Knob." Ashley received all the grateful hugs, then looked around for little Hannah, to find out David had already spotted her as he made his way by her side.

His big, beautiful smile stretched across his handsome face causing the five-year-old- to blink twice before giving him a smile.

"Hello Hannah. I know you don't remember me, but I was with your mama on the day you were born." His hand touched her long blonde hair as he remembered delivering the little bundle of love. "My goodness, has it been five years since I saw you open your blue eyes for the first time."

"My mama has blue eyes too, like mine." Hannah smiled shyly. "What is your name?"

"My name is David Reynolds, but you may call me, just plain David."

"O-key-do-key!" Hannah giggled as her tiny finger pointed up to the top of the tall tree. "Just plain David, I hung that beautiful shining angel up there!" Everyone laughed, including David when she said his name. She looked down, pouting, thinking those listening did not believe she placed the angel on. Her new friend David put her fears to rest when he lifted her up on his shoulders and let her touch the angel again.

"If anyone ever doubted your ability to hang the angel on top such a high tree, we just put that theory to rest, sweet Hannah." When she finally looked down, she saw his warm smile looking up at her. Ashley had walked over to join them and tell the small girl what had brought on the laughter.

"Hannah, I am your Aunt Ashley, your mama's twin sister and this is David, my very good friend."

"Hello Aunt Ashley. I really like your boyfriend." Hannah slid down and gave David a hug around his neck as he winked at Ashley.

Ashley reached out and touched his face tenderly as she kissed her adorable niece.

"David, you are a natural with children! You will make a great father someday."

"Only if I can have one certain someone for my children's mother!" Their eyes locked for a long moment before little Hannah started singing "Away in a Manger."

CHAPTER 11

Doctor David Reynolds came back with the lab report. Allison had a rare blood type and no one in the family, including her twin sister Ashley, was a match.

"Now what?" Dalton Lane clutched his Bible close to his chest. "I would have gladly given Allison one of my kidneys!"

Ashley had been observing the preacher's actions toward her sister ever since he arrived. His loving attendance by holding her hand, bringing her water, the way he looked at her. Ashley had seen the love between them as she reached over and touched his trembling hand.

"You are in love with Allison, aren't you Reverend Lane?"

"I have loved your sister for years, Miss Andersen, way before my best friend Joseph passed away." The preacher stood up and began pacing the floor. "Now, she may be dying if we cannot find a match in time."

"We mustn't give up hope, Dalton." Clara walked over and placed her arm around him. "Allison has her mother's blood type while Ashley got her father's. And just like her dear mother, Allison is a gifted artist. The blood type is rare, but not impossible to find."

"I have sent out an alert to the blood bank inquiring about any individual with her blood type who would be willing to give her a kidney." David Reynolds walked over next to his old friend, Dalton Lane and gently patted his back. "You are a man of faith, my friend, just keep hope alive inside that big heart of yours."

"David is right, Dalton, you do have a big loving heart." Clara smiled "You never revealed that strong love you had for Allison as long as your friend Joseph was alive. You performed their wedding ceremony and celebrated all their happy moments. When Joseph was so sick and had only weeks to live, you kept him supplied with the blood he needed to live. Joseph was more like a brother to you and you gave up your happiness for him." Clara looked deep into his eyes, to read more. "The truth is, you loved Allison Andersen the first moment you bumped into her at the train's station, when you arrived at Antler Knob to preach at your first appointed church."

"And that was way before your friend arrive in town, one year later." David had recalled the conversation while waiting for the fertilization results six years ago. "Why didn't you ask her to marry you Dalton, if you loved her so much?"

"I could ask you the same question, my friend, about one certain actress." Dalton couldn't help but smile, knowing he had put the doctor in a delicate position.

"It is different with me Dalton." David whispered, "Allison wanted to get married and have children, Ashley's career comes first with her and I did not wish to have the door slammed in my face."

Ashley had gone after Allison and tell her the latest results. They came out looking down cast, until Clara had a brilliant insight.

"Stop looking so gloomy girls! I have a hunch we will soon find that perfect match!" Clara winked at Bella, who was uncertain as to her meaning.

"David, I should have been a match for Allison! We are identical. We were conceived together and grew side by side! Is it possible she got mama's blood and my blood is like daddy's, just as Clara said?" Ashley had tears in her eyes as she looked up at the man she knew she had been in love with for long time. "We are so much alike, we could switch places without anyone knowing, remember?"

"I remember Ashley, but unfortunately Clara is right about your different blood type." David pulled her in close and gave her a hug. "Clara, do you know something we don't know?"

Ashley reached for Bella's hand. "Bella, you have a knack for knowing things. Can we hope for a miracle?"

"A miracle?" Bella's face was aglow when she answered. "Oh, yes! My dear friend, it is almost Christmas Eve, the night of miracles!"

Clara stood up smiling brightly as she announced, "I'm thirsty and I'm sure a holiday cup will cheer us up!" reaching inside her large bag, she pulled out a colorful flyer announcing a new holiday tavern in Antler Knob called Mistletoe and Holly. "It states here, come in to our grand opening and try our signature holiday cheer cup. It is guaranteed to warm your soul and lift your spirits with new hope for a magical Christmas!"

"I hear it's the best holiday cup around!" It was as though a little bird whispered that fact in Bella's ear as she added. "Now that you mention it Clara, I think a Christmas cup is exactly what's needed here." Bella joined her friend at the door. "We can finish our conversation at the tavern."

CHAPTER 12

The small group found the Mistletoe and Holly Tavern just one block from the clinic and waited until Allison called to check on Miss Gaston, the babysitter. She had fed the children and they were busy with the puzzle. All was well, so the mother of five could relax and enjoy her night out.

When they stepped inside the brightly decorated room with two large fireplaces at each end, they felt a sense of warmth. Familiar Christmas music was flowing throughout the candle lit room as a waitress walked up, dressed all in white with a brilliant smile on her sweet face.

"Welcome to our tavern. May I seat you at the large table by the Mistletoe fireplace?"

"That sounds perfect Brittany." Dalton read her name tag, flashing in bright blue lights. "The snow has started falling again and the warm fire looks most inviting, right gang?"

"You have a lovely place here, very festive." Ashley thanked David for pulling out her chair "And to be with the people we love, makes it perfect!"

"I could not have said it any better, my dear sister." Allison reached under the table and took Dalton's hand and whispered, "My hands need warming." Their eyes met and spoke volumes of love as he gently squeezed her hand.

Bella leaned over to her friend and whispered "Clara, Brittany came to work at the orphanage after Melody was called back. What is she doing here? Working in a tavern?"

"Bella, if you look around at the other workers, the bar maidens, the young singer at the piano, and the bartender, I'm pretty sure you will recognize them as well." Clara chuckled softly as her co-worker scanned the room to find Melody sitting at the piano singing "It's Beginning to Look a Lot Like Christmas", Samantha and Marigold tending tables as bar maidens and Bella gasp when the bartender turned around and smiled over at her.

"Simon?" Bella grabbed her mouth, sorry for her outburst, but to her delight everyone at their table was too busy chatting to notice her. She carefully whispered to Clara. "What exactly is going on here, Clara? And why are our friends all here working?"

Clara patted her back and smiled broadly. "You'll find out soon enough sweet girl. Now here comes our waitress. So just order a large cup of Christmas Cheer and enjoy it!"

"If that is what I am smelling in the air, I am quite sure I will!" Bella smiled at Marigold, who also wore a sparkling white dress and flashing white stars throughout her long chestnut brown hair.

"Are you fine folks ready to order? May I suggest our Christmas special, the Holiday cup, guaranteed to warm your soul and lift your spirits with new hope for a magical Christmas!"

"I shall have the large Holiday cup, with plenty of whipped cream!" Bella glanced down at the blazing fire to avoid the sudden attention from her group. Clara saved the day by ordering.

"Everyone could use something to warm the soul and lift spirits with new everlasting hope! Make mine a large Holiday cup also!"

"And trust me ladies, you will enjoy it till the last yummy drop." Marigold looked around the table and smiled so warmly, they could almost feel it touch their face. "Do I make it six large Holiday cups?"

"Why not! I say if Bella thinks it is worthy of making it a large cup, with whipped cream, then I'm in!" Ashley winked at her young assistant. "She didn't have to twist my hand when she insisted I try her coffee special, cappuccino. Now, that is my coffee of choice." The actress smiled up at the angelic face. "Please put this on one bill. My treat!" she looked around and noticed both men started to speak up, but with great flare, she waved them away, as though in one of her scenes "My money is made for my friend's enjoyment, therefore, I work, I strive for a better tomorrow, but to live without the joy of others, will make you a lonely, selfish, old woman!"

"I recognize that line from one of my favorite movies, Beyond Happiness!" A young woman seated next to their table jumped up, grabbing her napkin. "Miss Star, can I have your autograph?" she nervously held out the napkin. "Have you a pen?"

"I have a pen." Ashley pushed away the used napkin and pulled out a studio print then smiled up at her fan. "What is your name, my dear?"

"Lori Lawson, ma'am!" the girl blushed as the big star wrote something personal for her, then signed her name, Melinda Star, (Ashley Andersen) "You are Ashley? Allison's sister?"

"Why yes, I am. Do you know my sister?" Ashley looked over at her sister who was staring up at the girl, just as confused as she was.

"Oh yes, Miss. All the kids at the Angel of Mercy Orphanage knows all about you! You have been giving us things in your sister's honor for many years! That is how I got to see your movies, from the lifetime movie passes for the home kids. New furniture for every bed dormitory, a new dress for both Christmas and Easter for every girl and new suits for the boys! Money was sent for a better education and to help buy better meals. Because of your giving heart, the atmosphere and the attitudes have improved 100% and it has become a joy growing up in our home." Lori's eyes moistened with tears. "Now we might be asked to move. This might be our last Christmas at Angel of Mercy."

"I'm sorry if Lori is bothering you fine people." The matronly woman took a gentle hold on the girl's arm. "A couple of our girls work part time in here and invited the older kids out for hot chocolate, loaded with marsh mellows. Enjoy your drinks!" she pulled the excited girl back to their table as Marigold brought out six large steaming cups of holiday cheer.

Bella took sip after sip of the lovely tasting drink and looked up innocently when her group laughed at the whip cream over her top lip. Clara chuckled as she reached over to wipe off the white foam.

"Slow down girl! You will find there is a little kick in

Simon's cup of cheer." She whispered.

"Oh, but Clara, it's so lovely." Bella took another sip, extra careful this time as she declared "There's a hint of cinnamon, a pinch of nutmeg and cloves, and…" another sip to make sure, then her eyes lit up with revelation "I would say a good heaping tablespoon of ground up Cornucopia! That's what I smelled, of course, the Cornucopia flower!"

"I consider myself an expert in all kinds of flowers, Bella." Allison enjoyed the great tasting drink, as her eyes wandered to the table of home kids enjoying hot chocolate. "I have painted many different kinds of flowers and Ashley has given me several books on flowers as gifts over the years, and I have yet to see a Cornucopia."

"And I dare say you won't Allison!" Clara tried to laugh "At least, not on this earth. What is very rare on earth is plentiful in Heaven."

"Then how does Bella know what one smells like, much less taste like?" Reverend Lane sit up, anxious to hear her explanation.

"That is simple, Dalton. Clara and I have traveled through many countries over our lifetime and many places were just little out of the way spots, hard to find and harder to forget." Bella smiled over at her friend. "Right Clara?"

"That's right sweet girl, and it was on one of those unusual trips we happened upon the beautiful white flower with the most incredible smell and was offered a pedal for Bella's hiccups! It worked!" Clara took a big gulp when she added "A faraway place called Eden."

CHAPTER 13

Before anyone could remark about Eden, Bella jumped up, her eyes big as saucers, as she stuttered with her words.

"There…a …there is something…happening…!"

"Bella, are you alright, darling?" Ashley looked concerned as Clara stood up chuckling.

"Believe me, there is no need for alarm. I think Bella had a wee bit too much to drink and needs to be excused!"

"Excused? Where am I going, Clara?" Bella had the urge to wiggle about, feeling an unusual need, but not knowing what it was."

"You are going to the lady's room and use the…potty!"

"The…potty? Oh!" Suddenly a light came on in Bella's head as she realized what had happened. Bella's face turned red as she backed away trying to smile normally. "Excuse me!" she turned and dashed off to the rest room, quickly realizing God had given her the perfect match for Allison Andersen Stevens.

Before the group of young people left the tavern, the elderly lady walked back over after hearing Lori Lawson telling the group who the two twins were. She wrapped her old worn scarf tightly around her thin neck as she reached out and touched both twins' hands.

"Even though this may be our last Christmas together, the children ask me to thank you again for making their years at the home feel more like a real home and they will never forget your giving heart, Miss Andersen."

"Angel of Mercy was our home too, Miss Watson, and even though you apparently don't remember us, we will never forget your kindness and love." Ashley got up, along with Allison, to hug their old housemother. "Don't give up your hope for the home, Christmas Eve is a night of miracles, right Clara? Right Bella?"

Bella beamed with the good news she had to share later as she echoed Ashley statement.

Giving Hearts

"It is a fact, Miss Mable Watson, Christmas Eve is most certainly a night of miracles!" She looked around at her interested party. "I think I have found your perfect match Allison! Me!"

"That is wonderful news!" Simon walked over with another round of Holiday cheer for the six happy customers and a cup for each angelic employee, including himself. "Here's to warmth for the soul, a lift to your spirits and new hope for a Magical Christmas!"

With the warmth of the Holiday cup warming their bodies and the hope in knowing a Christmas miracle was not out of the question, both couples left with new hope in their heart.

As the group waited the test results from Bella's blood work, Reverend Lane walked in smiling, happy news of his own.

"I just left the choir practice and they are doing better than great!" he laughed as he slipped an arm around Allison. "Robin is a wonderful addition. Her young, yet mature voice blends in with the rest of the choir beautifully. I believe we stand a really good chance in winning the Christmas Eve contest this year!"

"You've just got to win this year Dalton. The Angel of Mercy is depending on you!" Allison touched his hand as she filled her sister in. "Every year a secret Santa gives 500,000 dollars to one lucky group of singers who come in first place in our annual Christmas Eve concert contest. Usually four to six groups compete, but the art school has many of their professional graduates to compete against our local churches and school groups, and always come in first place."

"I hear the judge is the same one every year, a Mr. Harvey Parsons, a talent scout from New York City." Ashley spoke up casually. "I think I read it from the Antler Knob Newspaper I receive once a month, just to keep up with home news."

Clara had been listening but had a question of her own. "Ashley, do you know this, Harvey Parsons? I just thought you might, being in the entertainment world and all."

"As a matter of fact, I have met the talent agent on several occasions." Ashley picked up a fashion magazine and flipped through it, to avoid direct eye contact with the cagy woman with the hardy laugh. "He seems very professional and charming and I am sure he chooses whom he thinks is the better performers."

"Ashley, you seem to know a great deal about a winning talent since you are number one at the box office." Dalton sat up with a brilliant idea. "Could you come and listen to our choir and give us a few pointers on the performing part, like our 'I'll Be Home for Christmas,' 'Jingle Bells,' 'Sleigh Ride' and a new original, written by our very own Robin Stevens, titled 'Christmas in Antler Knob.' We are asked to sing eight songs, so we picked four sacred carols. 'O Holy Night,' 'Silent Night,' 'Angels We Have Heard on High,' and another new original, written by myself, titled 'The Night of Christmas Miracles.'"

"Dalton, I never knew you could write music." Allison looked at him in amazement as she added "Come to think of it, I never knew Robin could write music either."

"I say the young lady inherited her gift for writing, just like her father." Clara's eyes twinkled when they fell on a surprised Dalton as Allison said, not catching the exchange looks between them.

"Joseph, a writer?" Allison looked confused, trying to piece together the connection.

"He did write that small article in the Antler Knob paper about building bird houses for spring, remember?" Dalton narrowed his eyes at Clara who was chuckling over the amateur article written by the young carpenter. "I recall the article was very informative."

"Since it was before Joseph and I really knew one another, I barely can remember the short article in the business section." Allison looked up at the door when David Reynolds and Bella walked out from the lab department smiling. "Good news?"

"The lab results are back and Bella is a perfect match! I would call that our first miracle and Christmas Eve is still four days away."

"God be praised!" Reverend Lane grabbed Allison and hugged her, then reached over to kiss Clara on her smiling cheek. "I don't know how you know things Clara, but Allison has a chance now to live her life."

"Doctor Reynolds, I've waited this long, can we postpone the operation until after Christmas?" Allison had everyone's attention. "It will be Christmas in four days and I've always been home for Christmas. Let me do this for the children, please. They need their mama."

"Excuse me David, but Allison this could get very serious if you put it off. God has given you a chance to live and I know those wonderful children would rather have their mama get well so she could be with them for many years to come!" Dalton's happiness over the good news turned swiftly to worry over the woman he loved so deeply. "Please Allison, reconsider this."

"David, would it endanger Allison's life if she put the operation off until after the holidays?" Ashley took his hands "Be honest with us, David, do we operate now or can my sister be with her children for the holidays?"

"Not the complete holidays, just through Christmas day." David patted Dalton on the back before knelling down in front of the sick woman. "Allison, you may spend the next four days with your children, but the first thing on December 26, you will be operated on and that is final! Understand?"

"Oh yes! Thank you, Doctor Reynolds! As long as I have Christmas Eve and Christmas day with my babies, I can go into that operating room with a peaceful heart."

CHAPTER 14

"Mama, Betsy Mason came to practice this morning coughing and sneezing, until the director sent her home to take something to make her well." Robin pulled her coat off and hung it in the closet. "Reverend Lane said ten members had called in feeling sick and ask for his prayers for healing."

"Nobody wants to be sick at Christmas, darling." Ashley glanced over at her pale sister and hoped David had made the right call. "Let's just hope Miss Mason didn't spread her cold to the choir with the concert only three days away."

"Oh, Aunt Ashley, we've just gotta win this year if we hope to save that beautiful old orphanage from being torn down!" Robin walked over to the window to check on her brothers and sisters building a snowman. "The town council says it must be condemned and torn down if it goes unrestored for one more year."

"The prize money is generous at 500,000 dollars, but for a building that size, it's only a drop in the bucket." Ashley stood up quietly, seeing her sister had drifted off to sleep, and walked over to collect Robin. She whispered. "Let's put on our coats and hats and go check out that snowman while you mama gets her rest."

Looking over at her sleeping mother, Robin nodded her head in agreement, and they got ready and slipped out the door where Clara and the other four children were laughing and throwing snowballs. A big fresh snowball smashed into Ashley's chest, causing her to laugh and start forming her own weapon, as she looked around to catch her assailant. Hannah tucked behind Clara when she realized she had missed her sister Robin and torpedoed her rich aunt instead.

Laughing over the funny situation, Robin pointed to the small five-year-old hiding.

"That snow bomb was meant for me Aunt Ashley! Little Hannah can't aim so good!"

"I see," tossing the perfectly made snowball to Robin, Ashley dodged other snowballs until she reached Clara, and gently pulled her out of the way. "There's my snowball princess! How would you like me to teach you how to make snow angels?"

"Wow! You can make angels out of the snow?" Hannah smiled brightly, glad she wasn't in trouble.

"Correction, little snowball princess, We, you and me, can make angels in the snow." Ashley lay down in the snow and Hannah followed. "Now, spread your arms out straight in the snow and slide them up and down, like this." When they stood up, Hannah looked down to see, two perfect angels in the snow, one big, one small.

"Those snow angels look almost like the real thing!" Clara chuckled at the images in the white snow. "At least they don't appear to be wings of bird feathers, but the gentle satin layers of real angel wings."

Ashley laughed and waved at Bella calling from the kitchen door holding up a cup.

"Everyone ready for hot chocolate and more talk about how Clara knows what kind of wings angels have?"

After Bella served the hot chocolate topped with marsh mellows, Ashley smiled at the cheery woman as she drank down the hot chocolate, then licked her lips. Clara turned to her and stated:

"Why would our loving creator put feathers on the angels when he was waiting to create birds and chickens?" she chuckled. "The angels were formed in God's image, just like humans, but for a different purpose. To serve Him in many different ways, with joy and praise! Right, Bella?"

"I could not have said it better Clara." Bella collected the empty cups as she smiled happily. "Wings of clear satin adorn the angels, that can be hidden for blending in with the humans, when on an assignment."

"If I didn't know better, I would swear you both are angels!" Ashley checked her watch. She had a call to make to California and there was a time difference, so she would wait a while longer. "Be honest, where did you find those facts on angels or are you just spinning a good tale for the children's sake?"

"Let me just say, it came from a good source." Clara smiled "And it gives the children something beautiful to dream about this night, right kids?"

"Right Clara!" Taylor and Tyler declared in unison.

"I hope I dream about snow angels and angels with clear satin wings, not chicken feathers!" Hannah announced.

"Billy, this is Melinda. Could I ask a favor from you? I know it's short notice but could you bring a small crew to Antler Knob and tape me making a pitch for a very good cause then take it to the television networks to reach fellow actors and other professionals. We need a Christmas miracle to save the home I grew up in!"

"Didn't your family home burn down when you were small?" Billy knew this actress felt compassion for many causes and he was always willing to do his part to help out. "Do you mean rebuild?"

"No Billy, that home was in Ashville, North Carolina. I'm talking about the orphanage I was placed in, along with my twin sister, when we were only five. Our home, the home we remember, is the Angel of Mercy Orphanage in Antler Knob, North Carolina. If we don't get the funds to restore it this year, it will be torn down."

"Antler Knob? Isn't that the town you secretly give 500,000 dollars to every year?" Billy remembered her generous gift to help out one winning group every Christmas Eve. "Why hasn't the town been using your beautiful gift to restore the old place?"

"The town did not get the winnings, Billy. The art school has won every year and due to the rules on who can enter, it is considered legitimate. To enter you had to live or work in Antler Knob at some time in your life. The professional singers who have left for broad way return to help the school win the prize."

"So, the art school chooses to keep the money for their needs every year instead of helping save the children's home."

Billy mumbled, knowing how unfair it really was. "Are none of the other participants any good? Does no one stand a chance against the art school?"

"The little Methodist church stands the best chance and have come in second every year, but there is only one prize." Ashley regretted letting Harvey Parsons set the rules and be the only judge. "I will be giving the group some pointers on their movements, to help their performance look more professional and they have one member of the choir who graduated from the art school, but decided to help her church this year. She might make it work."

"Too bad you can't carry a tune, Melinda. You might have saved the day for the church group." Billy teased.

"Very funny Billy!" Ashley laughed "Just be grateful I can act! You will send the crew, won't you darling?"

"I will personally bring them, along with some Christmas costumes for that Church group. They should look professional too. That is, if they are not planning to do all religious music and wear choir robes! This could be a turn off for that sour puss talent scout and his reason for not letting them win."

"Billy, I thought you like Harvey? You are the one who got him for me in the first place, remember?" Ashley smiled when she heard his familiar grunt over the phone.

"Stupid, that's what I was, real stupid! But it's not to late to let the best group win! Just tell me they are singing some regular Christmas songs." He crossed his fingers, in hopes of the right answer.

"Billy, do you have a problem with Christmas carols?" Ashley had hoped her friend wasn't like Harvey Parsons.

"Me? Heavens, child, I grew up singing all the beautiful Christmas carols! Silent Night, Away in a Manger! It's the times we're living in Melinda, we can't rock the boat!"

"Seriously! Billy, Antler Knob is a town of good people with faith, where we belt out 'Joy to the World' and 'O Come all Ye Faithful!' You can at least half relax Billy." Ashley chuckled, reminding herself of Clara. "The very talented church singers will be doing four beautiful Christmas carols and four regular Christmas favorites and I'm thinking about making it one more, 'Have Yourself a Merry Little Christmas!'"

"One of my very favorites! Too bad Judy Garland didn't live in Antler Knob at one time! Beautiful, simply beautiful!" he pictured the singer-actress singing to her stage daughter. "A sure winner!"

"Come down from that rainbow Billy, Judy won't be singing with our little group." Ashley laughed. "Now get busy packing everything and I expect to see you real soon."

CHAPTER 15

"It seems quiet here tonight." Dalton leaned back on the sofa, his arm resting around Allison. "I'm sorry you didn't feel like going to the Christmas play at the Tiny Theater on Elm Street. This is your first year to miss A Christmas Carol, isn't it?"

"I have sat on the second row, fifth seat, for as long as I can remember. The local talent always does such a wonderful job." Allison smiled up at the handsome preacher. "You should have gone with Ashley and David. The kids would have loved for you to go with them and Bella. Clara will look after me like an angel."

"Yeah! Like an angel!" The minister watched the cheerful woman come from the kitchen carrying coffee and cake. "She certainly knows how to bring out your smile."

"I always say, a happy person is already started on the road to recovery." Clara helped Allison sat up at her TV tray. "And Mr. Dalton did not go tonight because he didn't wish to miss 'our' fun and company, right reverend?"

"Well, you certainly know how to have fun, Clara." Dalton Lane ran his hand over Allison's hair "And I am truly with my favorite people."

"You have always cared for Allison, haven't you, Dalton?" Clara knew his great love for the sick woman and her love for him. She just needed them to finally admit it and now with the children gone, the time had come.

"I can't deny my feelings for Allison." His eyes met hers "I have loved you ever since we ran into one another at the Antler Knob Train Station when I first arrived in town."

"I don't understand Dalton. If you loved me, why didn't you ever tell me!" Suddenly Allison couldn't control her tears. "I was madly in love with you. From the moment our eyes met, I knew my heart belonged to you."

"And I felt your love for me, my darling, but Joseph came

into the picture and everything changed." He looked at her pleadingly, needing her to know the truth.

"I liked Joseph, he was a good decent man with a kind heart, but I wanted to belong to you, be your wife, have your children." She cried. "You pushed me into your friend's arms! Now that Joseph is gone, you confess your love for me! How can I believe you, Dalton? I won't let you hurt me again or the children. I fear they are growing too close to you already. Maybe we should not see one another anymore!"

"Reverend Lane, are you going to tell this girl the truth, or do you want me to?" Clara knew it was time for everything to come out, everything!"

"I'm the one that hurt her Clara. It has to be me to heal the wounds so our love can finally grow." Dalton took Allison's hands and looked her in the eyes. "I had just been given my first church assignment. A nervous stranger in a strange new town. I had been practicing my words for my first congregation as I got off the train. For a brief moment I closed my eyes and that is when I ran head on into the most beautiful woman I have ever known."

CHAPTER 16

Antler Knob, 1968

"Excuse me miss!" Dalton Lane looked down into the most incredible blue eyes in his world. "I do apologize."

Allison Andersen felt stunned for a moment when she stared up at the handsome stranger with black hair and green eyes. Finally finding her voice she said softly.

"May I suggest you keep your eyes open when you are walking in a public place." She smiled as she extended her hand. "Allison Andersen! And I except your apology Mister?"

"It's Reverend Dalton Lane and it is my pleasure to meet such a charming young lady on my arrival to Antler Knob." He sat down his luggage to shake her soft hand and noticed she had tears in her alluring blue eyes. "Is there a reason for your apparent sadness, Allison Andersen? I am a minister as well as a hopefully new friend."

"I just saw my twin sister off on the train that departed when yours arrived." She glanced down shyly, unsure of her sudden feelings for this handsome stranger. "Ashley is on her way to Hollywood, California in hopes of becoming a famous movie star."

"If she is identical to her sister Allison, she already has the looks for stardom." He gathered his luggage when he felt his stomach growl. "Tell me Allison, where can a stranger get a good meal around here? I am starving."

"Besides my own personal kitchen, you will find all our cafés and diners are wonderful." Allison couldn't control the butterflies that suddenly invaded her stomach as they walked toward the exit.

"Since you are here and probably haven't prepared for a dinner guest, which café or diner would you suggest we try first?" Stepping out onto the small town's sidewalk, Dalton got his first glimpse of the quant little town, lined with family owned businesses.

"We?" for a moment Allison felt forlorn panic. "Do you have family here? A wife maybe? Children?"

"No, just myself." He chuckled when she relaxed. "I was referring to us, you and me, having dinner together. After all, you are the only friend I know so far in Antler Knob."

Allison laughed, feeling happy and lightheaded as she led him down the clean sidewalk to a cozy Italian café, where white linen tablecloths covered each table, adorned with candles and red roses. Dalton looked around at the small, crowded room to find mostly couples, chatting softly over pasta, bread sticks, and wine.

"This looks like a popular place and the food smells heavenly." Dalton smiled down at the hostess who had observed the handsome stranger walk in with Allison Andersen, another home girl. "Table for two please. Lane." He looked around and saw a table in the far corner. "Could we have the table in the far corner?"

To herself she thought, you can anything you want, but openly she said, "Certainly Mr. Lane." She gathered up two menus and ushered them back to the corner table. "This is a perfect table for conversation. Enjoy your meal. Your server will be over shortly." As the hostess walked away, she mumbled to herself. "Oh, to be a server again!"

After ordering, Dalton smiled down at the girl he was certain he was in love with and would one day marry.

"Have you lived in Antler Knob all your life, Allison?"

"Most all my life I've called Antler Knob home." She smiled as the server poured two glasses of merlot then returned to the kitchen. "I was born in Ashville, several miles up the road. Our home caught fire in 1955, and my sister and I lost everything. Our home, our things, but mostly, our parents. We were only five years old."

"Sweet Allison, my heart goes out to you, in more ways than you could possibly know." Dalton reached for her hand, the love between them seem to flow right through. "Did you have relatives living here at Antler Knob?"

"We had just our grandmother Andersen and she was in a rest home, so she sent her personal aid to collect us and bring

66

us here to the Angel of Mercy Orphanage." Allison looked down at their joined hands and smiled. "It was a lovely place to grow up at, once we grew use to living with fifty other children."

"Fifty? What if it had been five hundred children?" Dalton released her hand when the server brought the food out. After she left, he continued "The reason I know what it's like to lose everything, is because I did as well."

"You were an orphan too?" She placed her napkin in her lap, looked up to see Dalton had his hands stretched across the table waiting for hers. Blushing, Allison took the preacher's hands so he could say a blessing. As the handsome minister twisted the pasta perfectly on his fork, he began his story.

"I lost my parents in an automobile accident when I was three and having no close relatives, I was placed in the Methodist Children's Home in Winston-Salem, North Carolina. I was a shy kid who was afraid of everyone and everything, especially cars." He glanced up and noticed Allison had fresh tears in her eyes. "It wasn't all bad. When I reached four, Joseph Stevens came to the home and he too was four years old, shy and afraid. We became the best of friends, more like brothers to one another. We enjoyed doing the same things, even playing sports. The only difference was, I excelled in football, baseball, and even basketball, but poor Joseph was always sickly and called by the other guys, a puny weakling. So, Joseph sat on the sidelines until he just gave up."

"Did he ever find a sport he could play?" Allison had her sister and the rest of the kids at Angel of Mercy were always supporting each other. She thought it must have been the amount of kids that made the difference. "Surely there was something your best friend could do well."

"He was the best in the entire orphanage when it came to woodwork. The woodworking teacher had Joseph help him in showing the slower boys how to hammer, saw, and build things, like bird houses." Dalton laughed when he recalled those days. "My birdhouse looked like a first grader had built it, and I was sixteen. Joseph's bird house looked better than Mr. Pavilion, our teacher's." Dalton thoughts took him back to the good times and the bad times. "Joseph and I always had each other's backs and I took on the role of being Joseph's defender and bodyguard and he was better with the fairer sex. All the girls seem to like Joseph, especially Alice Reid, a little red headed girl with emerald eyes, who all the other boys at the home had a crush on, including me."

"So, who finally won fair Alice's hand?" Allison smiled, trying to picture a bunch of young boys swooning over a red haired, freckled faced young girl. "Was it Joseph?"

"Only for a very short time." Dalton laughed as he recalled the embarrassing night. "Joseph found out I had a crush on her, so when Alice invited him over to her house to court on the porch, along with all the other girls living in that dorm, he pretended to get sick and sent me in his place. Needless to say, Miss Reid was offended and after giving me a few choice words, marched back inside the house, leaving me the laughingstock, standing there, looking really stupid, until my pal came and told the other boys off, causing their girls to go inside because all the girls respected Joseph."

"Those fellows could not have been happy with you and Joseph after that." Allison was drawn into his story and wanted to hear more. "Did they ever calm down and forget the incident?"

"Not for one second. Mitch Turner was the leader of that group and they set out to destroy us, any way they could." Dalton moved so the server could collect the plates. "One night when I was away playing football, Mitch and his thugs grabbed Joseph as he was leaving the girl's porch and beat him within an inch of his life. I found him all bandaged up in the infirmary when I returned. Some of the girls had heard the fight and called security. The gang ran before the men got there and they found my friend beaten and unconscious." Dalton stared from the window, his thoughts lost in another time. "I found my opportunity one night to get even. I waited out in the pouring rain for Mitch to leave his girlfriend, knowing he was always the last boy to go back to their dorm. He never saw me hiding in the bushes when I grabbed him in a choke hold and cut off his air. I commenced in beating the crap out of him and left him lying in the muddy ditch, the rain pelting down on his worthless body." His eyes met Allison's. "At least that was how I felt at seventeen until that Christmas Eve when I heard the Lord call me to the ministry and I confessed to Pop Woosley and was in the ditch digging every Saturday for four whole weekends. Then the good and gentle giant helped me get into Duke University's divinity classes after graduation."

"What happen to your friend Joseph?" Allison admired the person seated in front of her and she hoped he had feelings for her as well.

"Joseph had dreamed about becoming a pilot in the Air Force. He was turned down for medical reasons, so the only thing he cared about was carpenter work and got a good job for a local construction firm. He has saved his money and has enough to start his own company right here in Antler Knob. He should be arriving in about a month. He will stay with me at the parsonage until he gets his dream house built, in hopes of meeting the right girl and starting a big family." Dalton laid down a tip and helped Allison with her jacket. "Joseph has really thought this one out. He planes to show his home as an example of his fine work and reach out to all the towns in the area for business."

"Your friend sounds like he has his head on his shoulders too, just like you, Dalton." Allison followed him out the door. "I've put my application in several places, all of which are interested. Now, all I have left is deciding which job is right for me."

"May I make a suggestion, Allison? Until you decide which place is lucky enough to get you, why don't you come and help a friend move in. I know nothing about decorating and even though the parsonage is already furnished, I have my personal belongings that should have arrived before me." Dalton gently took her hand before picking up his luggage with his other one. "What do you say Allison Andersen, care to help a helpless bachelor start out on the right foot with his new congregation?"

"I would be more than happy to help my very good friend move inside his new home." They made their way down the street, keeping the tall Methodist steeple in view. They had already become close and their life together had just begun.

CHAPTER 17

Dalton unboxed his linens and towels as Allison arranged them neatly in the bathroom closet. His pots and pans were limited and he was virtually quiet as they worked until he unwrapped his coffee pot.

"Have I ever told you I make a great pot of coffee?" he turned it around in his hand as he checked it out. "Great! It wasn't damaged."

"I might warn you, I make a terrific pot of coffee." Allison laughed as she put away his plates.

"Think yours is better? I say we have a contest and find out." He helped her down from the step ladder. "Too bad we have only one coffee pot."

"Come over to my apartment Friday morning and bring your pot." Allison stood back to make sure she had everything arranged to suit her. "I'll fix breakfast." She smiled down at the shiny stove top, knowing hers could use a good cleaning. "Tell me Reverend Lane, are you ever going to use this stove or will it remain this clean and shiny?"

"I pride myself in cooking certain dishes, but by talent lies in baking." He knew he had caught her by surprise when she chuckled. "I will fix some of my secret cinnamon buns to bring Friday morning. They go great with 'my' coffee."

"Good! That means, they will go even greater with my coffee!" she enjoyed watching him laugh as she gathered up her bag and jacket. "Is nine o'clock alright with you, Dalton?"

"That sounds perfect, Allison." He walked her to the door. "Any decisions on which job you will take or are you still thinking?"

"I have come to a decision and I think it will make me very happy." She stepped out into the chilled mountain air. "I will be working as the Maple Grove Methodist Church's secretary, starting Monday morning." Allison beamed when Dalton's eyes lit up and a huge smile spread across his handsome face.

"I hope I can satisfy the new minister."

"The new minister could not be happier!" not wanting to let go of her hand, he asked "Got any plans Saturday night?"

"Not that I recall. How about you? Would you like to come over for dinner?" She loved holding his hand and wonder what it would be like to kiss him.

"I can't, I have a date." Dalton noticed her face fall, as she looked down. "That is, if I can persuade one Allison Andersen to go out with me to that romantic French Restaurant that sits at the end of town." Dalton couldn't keep from hugging her when she let out a long sigh. "Will you have dinner with me Saturday night?"

"I would love too. I haven't had the chance to try LeClair because the prices were out of my range. If you wish to change and go to Danny's burgers, I would not mind." She glanced down as she said so softly he could hardly hear her words. "As long as I am with you."

"I like being with you too, Allison and I want our first real date to be someplace special." He lifted up her face and their eyes locked. "I noticed the couple in the window at LeClair drinking champagne and kissing. They didn't need to say anything to express their feelings, it was just written on their faces."

"And in that kiss." The moment it slipped out of her mouth, she regretted having said it. Allison relaxed when Dalton burst into laughter, not from her words but from her innocence.

"It was a good kiss, Allison. I look forward to our first kiss." Dalton squeezed her hand, wanting to kiss her sweet lips right then and there but felt it too soon.

"It will be something lovely to look forward to." She hurried up the sidewalk, then quickly stopped, when he called her name.

"Which apartments and what number, Miss Andersen?" he stood smiling when turned back around "I would hate showing up at the wrong apartment holding an empty coffee pot and freshy baked cinnamon buns!"

"I would hate it even more, Reverend Lane. The lucky woman who opened the door would pull you inside, no questions ask!" Allison called back "The Winter Locks apartments, Holly Avenue, number 7." She waved "May the best pot win!"

"I've already won." He whispered to himself as he watched her turn the corner on Holly Avenue. I have found my true love!"

CHAPTER 18

Reverend Dalton Lane was right on time, nine o'clock sharp, coffee pot in one hand and freshly baked cinnamon buns in the other. As Allison opened the door, she thought to herself. You look tempting and delicious Dalton Lane, but her words came out simply:

"Mumm! Your cinnamon buns smell tempting and delicious!" She stood back so he could enter, a handsome smiled spread across his face. "Are you ready to start brewing?"

"I am ready for the challenge, Allison Andersen. Coffee pots up, lady and gentleman, let's start brewing!" The happy minister pretended to wave a flag as the pots were filled with water and measured coffee, plugged in and switched on. He laughed as he said, "Let the perking begin!"

"So far, both seem to be passing the smell test!" Allison carried four China cups to the table. "To get the most from any pot of coffee, you must start with the right cup."

"So, my Dixie hot cups won't work?" he teased.

"Only for emergency take out, Reverend Lane. Seriously, what do you use at your home?" Waiting to serve breakfast until after the taste test, Allison began pouring her coffee while Dalton poured his. She noticed hers was just a hint lighter. They took a seat in front of their coffee cups and began sipping slowly. They sat their cups down and looked at one another, then Dalton spoke up.

"I drink from my favorite mug at home. To be perfectly honest Allison, I think they are both great!"

"So, you are calling it a tie?" she waited for him to nod a positive. "And I would have to agree, 100%! We could open our own coffee house and call it Andersen-Lane or perhaps Lane-Andersen."

"If we wait awhile, we can call it plainly, Lane's coffee house." Their eyes locked as Allison wondered if he was talking marriage. Feeling somewhat uncomfortable, she stood up to get their breakfast out, along with his cinnamon buns. He watched her for a moment before getting up to refill their cups. "This really looks wonderful Allison. Being a good cook will be a plus." Dalton smiled and started eating and as promised, the cinnamon buns went wonderful with both brewed coffees. They spent most of the day together, just getting to know one another.

Saturday came, and Allison was on cloud nine all morning, thinking about her romantic date with Dalton. She was in love and she knew he loved her too after speaking around in circles referring to marring her. The call that would put a stop to her happiness came around noon when she heard a solemn Dalton on the other end of her phone.

"Allison, I regret I have to break our date tonight but Joseph arrived this morning and he is in a bad way. I cannot leave him like this. I hope you understand."

"Is he sick Dalton? Is there anything I can do to help you?" Allison felt like crying, but she wanted to sound brave and understanding with Dalton's dilemma. She had heard how close he and Joseph were, always there for each other. Much like her and Ashley. "I understand Dalton. Joseph needs his best friend." She closed her eyes as she added "Please call me later, this friend needs you too."

"I promise to call Allison, soon." Dalton closed his eyes as well, not wanting to betray his old friend when he needed him but mostly, for breaking the date he had been living for. "I'm not sure how long this will take, but don't give up on us, please."

"I will always be here for you Dalton. You are the one I want to be with, remember?" She felt some better by his last words. "Take as much time as you need, I'll be waiting."

"You are an angel, Allison Andersen! I am so blessed to have met you." He heard Joseph call out, as did Allison. "I need to hang up now, but I will call soon."

"I heard his call, Dalton. I understand, truly. Go to your friend. I'll be right here." She heard the phone go dead, laid her head on the table and let the tears flow.

Present time

"What had Joseph so upset that afternoon, Dalton?" Allison could not control her tears as he retold their love story and how it suddenly ended when his friend showed up. "You changed toward me that day, Dalton! I thought you love me the way I loved you!"

"I did love you, Allison, I have from the moment I saw you!" He tried to take her in his arms but she pulled away. "Allison, I do love you, very much! You of all people should understand what lengths a person will go to for their best friend, my soul brother, your sister!"

"Then tell me, what was so important to your friend that you would let him marry the woman you were ready to marry and destroy both our happiness?" Allison needed to know the reason Dalton would give up his love for his friend.

"Tell her Dalton, then let her mind and heart judge whether or not you did what you felt was right." Clara sat down between them, taking a hand of each. "The truth must be told if this love between you can survive."

CHAPTER 19

Saturday had arrived and I finished going over my sermon for the worship service. All was going to plan and my heart was singing with total joy, as I thought about you, my darling Allison and our romantic date. I had decided, even though it seem early, to confess my love to you at that little French Restaurant. I was standing at my closet trying to decide what to wear for the beautiful occasion when the doorbell rang and I saw Joseph standing on the porch, panic written on his face.

"Joseph! You are early. You said the end of the month!" He didn't say a word, but stood there shaking. "Hey buddy, what wrong with you?" I took his arm and pulled him in out of the wind, just in case he had fallen ill. He took a seat in the den while I made us a pot of coffee and fixed him a sandwich. He had managed to tell me he hadn't eaten for days, worried about something I was soon to learn.

"I got here last week Dalton, a little ahead of you, and got a room at the local inn." I could tell by the way Joseph devoured his sandwich; he was starving. "I finished earlier than I planned and decided to come straight here and start searching for a girl."

"What girl, Joseph?" I hadn't seen my friend since my summer vacation two years prior, when we managed to get away at the same time, so I wasn't sure what he was referring to. "Did you meet someone?"

"Yes, right here in Antler Knob, a year ago." He drank down his coffee, then refilled his cup and grabbed a cinnamon bun from our leftovers the day before. "She was the prettiest girl I have laid my eyes on. Long blonde hair, sky blue eyes and a smile that could melt anyone's heart." I was beginning to have a sinking feeling, hoping the description was just coincident and he was referring to another blue eyed blonde and not mine. So, I ask him:

"Where did you meet her Joseph?" I needed to know. "And

why were you in Antler Knob in the first place? It's a long way from Winston-Salem.

"The construction firm I worked for sent me and two other carpenters here to build new bookcases for the local library." Joseph thought back to arriving in the small quant mountain town. "It had already grown cold up here and they had their first snow fall of the year. I told the fellows I could understand why this town would decorate so early for Christmas, then learned later it was a Christmas town. They hold two big events that bring in lots of tourists and much needed income for all the family-owned businesses. One celebration is called: Christmas in July at Antler Knob. The other, which last the entire holiday season, is called: The Season of Lights, and its big attraction is the Christmas Eve Concert, featuring many different groups."

When my friend told me about the Christmas Eve Concert, it hadn't become a contest yet. But the following year a secret Santa changed it forever. Then I continued to listen to Joseph as he related how he met this girl he was madly in love with.

"We arrived at the library and were shone to a big warehouse next to it. We were to measure the old cabinets, build the new ones in the warehouse, then tear down the old and replace them with the new. There was an orphanage nearby who had sent a small group of girls to remove the books and placed them neatly in an orderly manner. That was the first time I saw her. There were ten girls, but I saw only one, my Ali." I closed my eyes and knew we had fallen in love with the same incredible young woman. As I listened to my friend going on about 'his' girl, my heart was breaking, knowing I would have to make a decision that would affect the rest of three lives forever.

"Ali, short for Allison, had a sister named Ashley, a twin. The fellows couldn't believe I could tell them apart because they looked identical, but I could tell, see a big difference. In their personalities and how they were with the other girls as well as the little school children that came in to be read to. They always wanted Ali. She was a natural with the children and I knew she would make a great mother one day and in my dreams, I thought, a mother to my children." For a while he looked as though he were reliving those moments with you as he continued his story, a peaceful smile upon his lips.

"Unlike the other nine girls, Ali never offered to flirt with either of us. Besides me, there was Daniel, a really great looking guy with blonde hair, whom one of the girl's nicknamed Tab, for Tab Hunter, the dashing young actor. Curtis was short and a bit overweight and the only girl interested in him was a short, overweight gal named Martha Mae." I remembered Joseph stopped to laugh, not in a mocking way, but in a, but at least he got his girl, way, because he added "They hit it off really well. Before we left for home, Curtis was engaged to Martha Mae and they got married after her graduation." I had to know if anything happened between him and my girl, so I ask "Did you find the courage to ask Allison out?" I had said your full name from habit, but Joseph was so caught up in the past, he never noticed as he answered in a dazed.

"Ali had brought me and the fellows some hot chocolate one afternoon. The temperature had dropped down in the low twenties and all that the warehouse had for heat was a single wood burning stove, that ate up wood as fast as Curtis ate up the Krispy Kreme doughnuts Martha Mae would bring him." He laughed. "She said the hot chocolate might warm us up so we could do our work without shaking. I didn't need any hot chocolate to warm me up when Ali was around. The light that reflected from her beautiful soul radiated my entire being and I knew I was in love.

I think her sister Ashley had a thing for me, because she would bring me little things belonging to her that needed fixing. A jewelry box with a broken hinge, a small stool that needed the legs made tighter and a mirror stand that was missing some nails. Instead of helping with the books, Ashley would sit on my toolbox, laughing and talking about silly girl stuff. The guys knew I was crazy about Ali, but couldn't understand why I wouldn't settle for her identical twin Ashley, since it was obvious she had a crush on me." I remember Joseph's eyes when he looked up into mine, with all the seriousness of saint. "Dalton, they could never understand my real feelings for Ali. I loved that girl so much I could see right through to her very soul. I knew she liked me, a lot. Even agreed to let me take her to a movie a couple of times and…" he blushed before adding "She permitted me to give her a goodnight kiss before I drove her back to the girl's dorm room on our last date. There were several occasions when she arrived with either, coffee, hot chocolate, or hot spiced apple cider. She was our little angel of mercy and my one true love."

"Did you ever tell Ali that you loved her?" I had to know and mostly how you responded.

"I did find the courage. We had completed our project and would be headed home the following morning. That was the day of our last date, I spoke about." Joseph swallowed, as though he were going to tell you all over again. "After our kiss, I was ecstatic and knew I needed to tell Ali how I felt before she got out of the car. So, as soon as I put the car in park, I draped my arm around her shoulders and told her how much I loved her and it would make me the happiest man alive if she would be my bride!"

"The happiest man 'alive' kept going through my head, over and over and I almost missed his last response when he added softly. "Ali could only stare at me, either not sure how to answer or too sweet to hurt my feelings. I remember her taking my hand before climbing from the car and speaking. She said, 'you are one of the sweetest, most gentle, and loving friend any girl could wish for. I like you Joseph, I like you very much and I always hope we can be friends in this life. I'm just not ready for a commitment right now Joseph, I hope you understand.' Then she gave me a beautiful smile before adding 'Please keep in touch. Goodbye Joseph and have a safe trip home."

"So, you are here looking for this Ali and if you should find her, what will you do if she still says no?" I wasn't sure what frame of mind my friend was in because I had seen him sent away before to a mental institution for another break up, that appeared to be small compared to how he felt about you. That's when Joseph broke down in sobs and kept repeating:

"She has got to say yes! Ali must say yes! I will build her a home! I will give her lots of babies! I will love her till I die!" Then I ask him again. "And If she says no, will you stay here or find another town to start your new company?" I still had hope for a future with you, my darling Allison, but I needed to know my best friend would survive.

"If Ali says no...I will..." his face fell in his hands, weeping out of control as he mumbled in defeat. "I will kill myself! I don't want to live without Ali! I'd rather die and forget my stinking miserable life ever existed!" It was at that moment I knew I had to tell him where you were and help him win your love.

"But why couldn't you just tell him how much you loved me? Did you have to destroy our future so he could find the happiness he wanted?" Allison wanted to find a reason for the man she loved since that day at the train station, but it appeared he thought more about his friend's happiness than he had his own or hers. "I know you loved Joseph! I know you both had a lousy childhood, for the most part, I realize the closeness you felt, I felt the same thing for my sister, but I would never permit Ashley to come between you and me?"

"Allison, you might have given up all your happiness for your sister if you found out she had only a few years left to live." Clara knew the truth and Dalton needed to tell Allison everything so she would understand and find the forgiveness she so desperately longed for.

"Alright Allison, I will tell you everything and I must warn you, there are things that will change your world for good." Dalton took a deep breath and chose his words wisely.

CHAPTER 20

"Sometime back when I was in Duke, a chaplain from the Air Force made a talk to my class about the trauma new recruits face when entering. Men with little or no faith at all had the hardest time, but he found men who wanted to in list and were turned down for medical conditions had the hardest time. These small group of men felt inferior to the healthy soldiers and couldn't understand why high blood pressure, heart conditions, or being too short or too thin, kept them out, when they were willing to fight, even give up their life for their fellow air pilots or their country. After the talk, I cornered Chaplain Baker and asked him if he remembered a young fellow named Joseph Stevens. He just stared at me for a long while, then pulled me to one side, keeping his voice low.

He said he remembered Joseph Stevens well. He had talked with him at length, trying to reassure him his health issues shouldn't keep him from doing the things he wanted, just not any military service. After several sessions with Mr. Stevens, he seemed well enough to move on. Then he asked how I was connected to Joseph and I told him about our friendship and growing up at the children's home. He asked me if Joseph had ever told me why he was put in the orphanage in the first place and I honestly did not know. Joseph never wanted to talk about his past, so I respected his wishes, so Mr. Baker told me the reason.

Joseph was from an abusive family. His parents were on hard drugs and strong alcohol. Even while his mother carried him in her womb, she drank, smoked and took the drugs, leaving poor Joseph addicted even before he was born. Some neighbors found him lying in the mud, unconscious, beaten black-and-blue and half-dead. The only reason they knew the child was living was his uncontrollable jerking. Little two-year-old Joseph was high on drugs, malnourished, and weighed only ten pounds. The parents were arrested for child abuse and died a year later from a prison overdose. It took Duke Hospital two years to wing the small boy from the drugs and build up his strength, almost losing him four times. When he got released, he was placed in the Methodist Home for Children. I stood there, trying not to get emotional, but my heart was breaking inside and I still hadn't heard the worst. He told me there was more, something he hadn't even shared with Joseph, but he wasn't sure he should tell me, since I wasn't kin. I then convinced Chaplain Baker Joseph was my soul brother and we were the only family between us, so he told me.

Under the old shade trees on the campus, sitting together on an old oak bench, the chaplain told me my dearest friend in all the world was dying and had only twelve to fifteen years left. This is why when Joseph declared if you married him he would be the happiest man alive. Then moments later, Joseph said, I will love her till I die. He had laid out his reason for winning your hand. To makes his last few years happy, you would have to be a part of them so he could love you until he died!"

Tears swelled up in Dalton's eyes, remembering being torn between making his own life complete and happy with Allison or sacrificing his happiness so his friend Joseph could have his last few years on this earth filled with the joy he had always been searching for. If then he remained a bachelor, then maybe he and Allison could have a life together one day.

Allison stood up and walked around Clara and stood in front of Dalton, tears running down her beautiful face. Now Allison was the one that was sick and may be dying if the transplant failed. The cold reality hit both of them as Dalton stood and gathered Allison in his arms. Clara smiled to herself, knowing all would work out now for this perfect couple. She placed a warm hand on them both and with a radiant smile said:

"I see a perfect match! Both with giving hearts, putting other's needs before their own. Gathering rain and spreading out rainbows, picking up an empty stem and filling it with fragrant pedals. I see a beautiful long marriage and a lot of happy children, with loving parents."

Allison and Dalton had been listening in wonder at Clara

heavenly revelation and both felt their heart leap with new hope for that Christmas miracle.

"But Dalton, before we start celebrating, I think there's more to the story and the other big gift you gave Joseph, after he learned he was dying."

"What gift Dalton? The fact that you pushed us together, performed the ceremony when we got married, was there to celebrate each anniversary, bless each baby when they arrived?" Allison knew all this and why she finally said yes to Joseph's proposal. She had assumed Dalton never loved her in the first place and just considered her a good friend. Feeling betrayed, Allison had resigned from the secretary job at church, even before her first day and declared she had a better offer, working for Joseph as the company's secretary. The sad truth was, she couldn't bare being around the man she had given her heart to and watch him around other women. Now, once again, Allison waited for another truth.

CHAPTER 21

"Allison, you and Joseph tried to have a baby and it appeared hopeless until at last you got pregnant only to lose the baby at two months. Your doctors suggested you both have a test and find out if there might be a problem with one of you. You were told it would not be safe for you to carry a baby full-term, if at all, and it could be life threating. Joseph had told you he checked out fine, but he was only sparing you from the hard truth. His doctor found the rare blood disease that had kept Joseph out of the Air Force and it affected his sperm where he could not ever have children."

"Not have children? I don't understand!" Allison walked away and looked up at the family painting, Joseph smiling in the center, healthy and happy. She never painted him the exact way he looked right before he died, she painted him from memory when they were first married. "Joseph donated his sperm to fertilize the eggs I supplied. We had five beautiful healthy babies. As you very well know, Reverend Lane."

"I am more aware of that fact than you know, Mrs. Stevens!" Dalton looked down when Clara took his arm. "Do I tell her everything Clara? I promised Joseph she would never know."

"Under the circumstances Dalton, I think your best friend would want you to share this news with the woman you have always loved. Joseph loved you too and would do anything for you, remember. Giving up his Saturdays with that little red head to work alongside you in that dirty ditch." Clara chuckled "As I recall, that was when he lost her to Alfred Cook."

"You're right Clara. Joseph had no way of knowing how much I loved Allison. Had he known, he would want her to know who fathered her children." Dalton walked over next to Allison and turned her around to face him "Alright Allison, you want to know the real facts, then I will tell you. Joseph isn't the father of your children, I am!"

"You?" The truth fell on her like a heavy burden was lifted

away from her heart. "Robin, Tyler, Taylor, Jonathan and Hannah are...Your children?"

"They are our babies, Allison Andersen Stevens!" he felt relieved when she at last broke into a beautiful smile. "Joseph came to me after seeing the doctor and told me he had a blood decease that kept him from having babies and that was the one thing he had promised you. To give you a house filled with happy children. Then he shared with me the fact that the doctor had told him he only had ten to twelve years left."

"How was he? Did he fall apart like before?" Allison's heart was breaking for the man she had lived with, surprisingly happy, for fourteen years.

"No, he was actually calm about the whole thing. Now that I recall his words, I wonder?" Dalton paused, remembering the conversation. "He looked at me with the most loving expression and said, I want you to be the father of Allison's babies. This is what I want! This is what Allison would have wanted if she could have chosen for herself and this is what you have been missing. I know, I've watched, I've witnessed. Dalton, you are the best friend a man could ever have and because of you and your unselfish giving heart, your loyalty has always remained constant. There's no need to worry about me anymore. I'm not afraid to die, so now I just want you to start living again. You gave me what I needed to make me the happiest man alive for as long as I live, and I have been and will be as long as I breath. But I want my Ali to be happy and complete and this means having children, lots of children. Please do this for Allison and her true dreams will finally began to come true."

Dalton walked over by the Christmas tree, remembering decorating it with the children, his children, then lifting his youngest up to place the angel on top. The joy he felt in her hug and bright smile and the pride he felt watching his first born sing her first solo from her own beautifully written song. He so wanted to be a part of this family he helped bring into the world the only way he could. Now, he thought, he and Allison could have another baby, but this time through the act of their long-awaited love.

"Tell me, Reverend Dalton Lane, what is going through that

wonderful mind of yours?" Allison had walked up behind him and looped her arms around his waist.

"I am thinking what a wonderful life it would be to finally be a part of this family. To be the children's daddy and to at long last, be your loving husband." He swooped her up in his arms. "Oh, get better my darling so we can get married and have another baby, the normal way."

"I would like nothing more, Dalton, my dearest love." Allison had never felt so much happiness "You know what the doctor told me and now that I have to have a new kidney, I may never have any more children." She kissed his sad face "But cheer up, we already have five beautiful children."

"I always say there's room for one more and six is such a lovely number." Clara had been listening but could not keep quiet another second. "There is no reason you cannot have a baby, Allison, the normal way, of which I know nothing about but hear it's quite nice for human couples. I say you two have waited long enough, so as soon as that new kidney arrives, get hitched and have a long honeymoon, bringing back good news! I'll hang around to watch those beautiful babies you've already made and spoil them a little more while you're away having fun. Or so they say."

"Clara, I don't know how you know the things you know, but we love you!" Dalton laughed, still holding on to his true love. "You are a hoot!"

"Well, thank you! Owls are wise, or so I've been told." She chuckled. "Now that we have you two straighten out, what do we tell the children, when and how much?"

"Miss Clara, I am totally surprised at you!" Allison laughed, along with Dalton. "I thought you had all the answers."

"Oh, I do. I was just hoping you two knew." Clara picked up the empty cups and laughed "Better think of something soon. I see a wedding, no two weddings, on New Years Day and time for chit chat is over for this night because those precious babies will be coming in that door any minute." She chuckled as the door flew open and Hannah rushed inside excited about the play and shared her excitement with her mama and her good friend Dalton.

CHAPTER 22

Ashley had been waiting in front of the Angel of Mercy Orphanage with David and Bella. Her reliable director would be arriving on schedule and then she could tape her announcement to her fans and fellow actors. The big black limousine pulled to a stop right in front of the beautiful actress and her robust director climbed out from behind, along with a camera man and Mrs. Vera Sanders, the dance instructor for many of the M.G.M. musicals. Billy met Ashley with a big fatherly hug.

"We are all here!" he chuckled "Is this where you grew up Melinda? A lovely old house."

"That is the description I would have used Billy, a warm home." Mrs. Sanders smiled at the star. "I hope you don't mine my tagging along with Mac." Her nickname for the cheery director. "He said I might be of some assistance with that church group."

"Well, I'm sure you can teach them better moves and dance steps than I can, Vera." Ashley laughed "I think I was born with two left feet."

"Then you make up for it in your great acting." The dance instructor liked Melinda Star and found her warm and friendly toward everyone. "What you lack in singing and dancing is certainly made up in your drama and even comedy. You, my dear, are a natural."

"That is most kind of you Vera. I'm sure Reverend Lane will welcome you with open arms." Ashley turned to her director. "Is the camera in the car or coming in a truck. We need to get going so the stations you got can show my tape tonight."

"My dear girl, do not underestimate this big guy. I persuaded every major networks to air your plea. Millions will hear what you have to say. As for the camera, it will be arriving on the truck any second." The sound of a big tracker trailer could be heard coming down main street and within seconds, it came into view. "And there's our truck." It pulled to a stop. M.G.M. written in bold letters on the side.

"Seriously! Billy! A big rig for one little camera and a few costumes?" Ashley narrowed her eyes at the laughing man. "Billy I'm almost afraid to ask, but what else in inside that big truck?"

"Christmas props and lights from holiday musicals." Billy noticed her worried look, so before she could voice her doubts, he laid them to rest. "Just calm yourself down, Melinda, and listen to the expert. I telephoned Mr. Parsons when I found out by a secret source that the art school group had been using props from Broadway shows in New York and he was secretly giving them the green light, against all rules. Facing being called out and fired, if you will, from various projects I helped him obtain, he agreed to let the church group use any props available."

"Billy, you are a genus, except for one small hic-up." She patted his questionable face. "The stage is not big enough for every act to sit up an elaborate set! I'm told the art school already takes up half of it."

"Are you finished?" he arched his eyebrow. "I ask Mr. talent agent how large the stage was and how many entrants would be performing this year. The cocky little jerk said, due to the art school always coming in first, most of the groups dropped out this year. Then the little devil laughed as he stated only one act was left to compete against the winners, the pathetic little church group."

"Then if he is bias, inclined to be one sided!" Melinda frowned "It's my contest! I pay the winnings! I say we need another judge."

"I say we need three judges my dear." Billy, grew close to the star and whispered, "The rules will have to be for all judges to vote unanimous and the little jerk will think twice before voting against me, Harvey, and you, my dear."

"I'll do it!" Melinda kept a serious face as she added "We must be honest and fair Billy. The best group will be awarded the prize."

Giving Hearts

"My fellow actors and my dear devoted fans, I am speaking tonight on behalf of those children who have no families to spend Christmas with this year, or any of their growing up years. They are orphans and they miss out on many things we take for granted. Home and family, gathering around the table and having Christmas dinner, then opening presents and singing carols around the big, beautiful tree in the living room. Trying desperately to fall asleep so Santa wouldn't catch you awake, then waking up on Christmas morning to find the presents Santa brought. What a magical feeling! But an orphan is surrounded by many other orphans and life for them is so different, yet in most cases, there is a lot of love.

Most of you know me as the actress, Melinda Star, but I was born Ashley Andersen, along with my very best friend and identical twin sister, Allison. We were only five years old when our daddy carried us from our burning home and went back inside to get our mama. We never saw either of them again. They perished in the fire and we were taken to an orphanage in the small town of Antler Knob, North Carolina called The Angel of Mercy Orphanage. It became our home and all those working there seemed to really be angels to all the children they devoted their life to. Most of you remember the home you grew up in with loving parents and brothers and sisters. We orphans remember our home too and now I have found out my beautiful home will be torn down if it is not restored back to code. This beautiful old building behind me is my home, the one sited for demolition, if funds are not collected to restore the property and bring it up to today's standards.

The Methodist church in Antler Knob hoped to win the Christmas Eve Concert contest which will receive $500,000, and I plan to match that amount with another, 500,000. I have spoken to the man restoring the building and he says to completely restore it will require five million dollars. I am asking everyone who can to give whatever they can to help. Not for me, but for the children and youth who call Angel of Mercy home. If this beautiful old home is torn down, these children will be placed in foster homes, separated from their sisters or brothers and the property will become another shopping mall.

I pray that you will feel the spirit of Christmas and open up your hearts and wallets so these children can enjoy many more Christmas's in their home. May each and everyone of you have a very blessed Christmas and the happiest of New Years! Thank you and God bless!" The camera light went out and Billy gave her a thumb's up as he said, "I pledge 500,000 dollars, my dear!" He winked at her. "I have a hunch you will bring in enough funds to restore several children's homes in N.C." He motioned the camera man away as he kissed Melinda's cheek. "I'm off to design the set. I have someone meeting me at the auditorium to show me the stage set up. This little town hasn't seen a set-up like this since Bing Crosby's 'White Christmas!' Hurrah for Hollywood!" Billy chuckled as he danced happily to the long car.

"Ashley Andersen, you are a jewel!" David lifted her off the ground and twirled her around. "You never stopped amazing me with your giving heart."

"You're pretty special too, Doctor Reynolds." Ashley hugged his neck, laughing. "Don't you think I've noticed all those different charities you gave to when you have asked me to deliver your mail to the post office. After seeing the top two charities, I couldn't help but see what else you give to, or…" she glanced up teasingly. "A letter or card to a female I wasn't aware of."

"Checking up on me, ah!" David goosed her side, causing her to giggle.

"I have to keep my eyes on what my fellow is up to when I'm busy working." Ashley motioned for Bella, who had been listening from a short distance away, pretending to be checking out the beautiful old rose garden, frozen with snow and ice sickles. "Bella, could you grab my purse and I'll take two of my favorite people out to lunch."

"That sounds lovely, Ashley. I am rather hungry and forgive me, David, but I did hear your tummy growl when our beautiful movie star was giving her sales pitch." Bella tried to keep a straight face when the handsome doctor grabbed his stomach and laughed. "By the way Ashley, it was a grand speech and I do believe you will exceed your goal, just like Billy predicted."

Giving Hearts

"If there is an outpouring of support and we do exceed the amount we need, reaching out to other orphanages who need their homes restored is a greater blessing still."

"There are new miracles occurring every day as we grow closer to Christmas Eve." David took both the ladies' hands and headed down the sidewalk toward the eating places. "It's a wonderful feeling knowing things are getting better and we can see that light at the end of the rainbow."

"It's more like, things always get better when we can see that light at the end of that long dark tunnel." As Bella beamed with the vision of Heaven, Ashley and David could only assume she was just rephrasing his words to something more down to earth, as they smiled at one another.

CHAPTER 23

"There's a phone call for you Reverend Lane." Robin had been waiting by the telephone for her friend Mandy Montgomery to call about the birthday party Mandy's mother was giving her daughter. Being born December 23 made it so close to Christmas, that everyone was busy with Christmas activities and holiday parties, Robin included. Practice had become an everyday occurrence and if the party was planned during her much-needed practice, Robin would simply have to decline the invitation and miss out on some really cool fun and food. She handed the preacher the receiver, praying silently that his call would not take long.

"Reverend Lane here." Silence meant the caller was relaying a message on the other end, then Robin noticed the anxious face on her minister as he continued to listen. "Let's hope Doctor Robinson can give them something to make them well for dress rehearsal or a least for the night of the performance!" he listened for a minute longer before concluding "If they don't get better, we will have to work with the ones we have left. I'd ask Allison, but my poor darling isn't feeling well herself, and…" he winked teasingly at the young girl, who blushed because he caught her checking her watch a third time. "I'm not certain she or her twin sister Ashley can carry a tune." He noticed Robin chuckle and he didn't feel too guilty for admitting it. "Look, I have someone here expecting a very important call…" listening to the caller, then "yes, yes, I know this is a set back Ronnie, but it can't be helped. I will see if I can round up some singers. Try to calm down! Things will work out on the night of miracles!" silence meant talking on the other end. "Yes Ronnie, I truly believe that things will work out. We will get that Christmas miracle."

"That was Ronnie!" Dalton made his way back inside the den and took his seat next to Allison. "Being the choir director comes with loads of responsibilities and a great many upsets, including choir members who come down with a bad sore throat or worst, laryngitis."

"Please tell me you are not saying one of our choir members won't be able to sing Christmas Eve? It's times like this I would give anything if I could carry a tune so I could just fill in the empty spot..." Allison laughed sheepishly. "That is, if it was a woman sick."

"You can paint circles around all those songbirds, sweet girl." Clara walked from the kitchen carrying coffee and homemade sugar cake. "Five singers! Coming down with the same thing at the same time!" she clicked her lips as Allison sat up. Eyes wide.

"Five? We have lost five singers with some kind of sore throat?" Allison took a small bite, then thought of Robin. "Dalton, you don't suppose my little girl might come down with this sick throat and miss her first concert?"

Dalton reached over and rubbed her stiff neck as he spoke softly, just for her and Clara's ears. "Robin, our lovely daughter will be fine and Ashley called me earlier at my office and said if I needed a few more singers, she found six young people, juniors and seniors from the Angel of Mercy who had great voices as well as Bella, whom she caught singing in the kitchen. If you need a soloist, Bella's your girl!" Dalton noticed Clara chuckle, so he added "And maybe Clara can sing with our group."

"I do love singing, reverend, but I just might need to share my talent of piano playing for the concert."

"Now that is funny Clara! Why on earth would a piano player have to drop out due to a sore throat?" Dalton chuckled at the thought.

"Because, he isn't getting a sore throat reverend, he still has to put up the outside lights on his rooftop. His wife has been after him for over two weeks and her big neighborhood Christmas party is tomorrow night." Clara casually took a sip of coffee, then peered up over the cup's rim. "Are you getting the picture yet? The ladder has been up for a week, waiting for the not-so-sure foot, piano player." Clara stood up to open back the curtain, revealing the latest snowfall, silently coming down on the four youngest children, trying hard to catch the flakes on their tongues. "Beautiful white snow can be dangerous if one is standing on a high steel ladder reaching up to hook on Christmas lights in a hurry. One wrong move and…" Clara looked toward the telephone as it rang out. "Luther Lambert will slip and fall. Two, broken wrist can make playing a piano impossible."

Dalton and Allison stared at the woman who seem to know everything, even before it happened and once again Robin called the preacher to the telephone.

"It's Ronnie, Reverend Lane." Robin held her hand over the mouthpiece and whispered. "I think he's crying sir, or at least that's what it sounds like."

"I would not doubt it, Robin. When things get tough, Ronnie can get emotional." Dalton couldn't understand why Robin was the only child they had who called him Reverend Lane or sir. The other children had always called him Dalton, especially little Hannah. He longed to hear them call him daddy, but that might take some deep thought as to how he and Allison might approach telling them. Taking the phone, Dalton listened to a panic choir director relating the latest bad news. The piano player had indeed fallen off the ten-foot ladder, and, trying to catch himself with his hands, broke both wrists.

"Calm down Ronnie, it's not the end of the world." Dalton tried to reassure the upset director, but he wasn't hearing any of it.

"Not the end of the world? Then tell me Reverend Lane, what else has to happen to make you give up on this fake hope of our winning the contest?" he was practically yelling. "Tell me so I will understand your cool calmness over this tragedy!"

"Ronnie, there's no need for all your dramatics! We have so far seven highly qualified singers who can join our group and one angel of a piano player who is more than willing to take over the bench." Dalton continued sympathetically "Ronnie, if you have faith the size of a mustard seed, miracles will happen. All you have to do is just believe, then sit back and enjoy the hand of God."

"Thanks Dalton, I feel a whole lot better." He gave his

minister a weak laugh "I just hope I don't get another stressful call or you might be praying for a choir director when I end up having a nervous breakdown."

"I'll let you know if Clara sees anymore mishaps and call to warn you." Dalton chuckled, knowing he had the director baffled. "Relax Ronnie, I've not gone off the deep in. Just wait until you start working with her and don't worry, you will enjoy every minute with our charming Clara."

As Dalton related the news about the piano player falling, just as Clara had predicted, the phone rang again. This time it was Robin's friend calling about the birthday party. After hanging up, Robin came into the den to report her good news.

"Mandy said her party was going to be tomorrow morning, at ten o'clock. She knew I would be having dress rehearsal all afternoon tomorrow, even into the evening if we needed more time." Robin was aglow with the good news and her friend had made sure the time suited Robin and it appeared all the other invites could attend as well. "Mandy said her mother had her birthday cake made in holiday colors, with icing holly and berries adorning the top. The vanilla ice cream had been ordered directly from the creamery and dyed red and green."

"That sounds like the perfect birthday cake for someone born so close to Christmas." Clara placed a cup of hot spiced apple cider in her young girl's hand. "If it's a Christmas theme, are you supposed to wear a holiday dress?"

"I guess I'll wear the same one I wore last year, if it still fits." Robin knew her mother's sickness had drained most of their savings and not being able to work, her daddy's small insurance check could only stretch so far. Asking anyone for help was very difficult for Allison, even her twin sister, who she knew would offer her any amount she needed if she knew their situation. The only one who knew, Robin admired and respected. Dalton Lane would do anything for them and it was obvious to the twelve-year-old, he was in love with her mother. She had also witnessed just how much her mother loved him and had hoped some day they would get married so she could finally stop calling him Reverend Lane or sir and use his real title, daddy. Young Robin Stevens had been putting things together and figured out the truth. Her eyes met the man she wanted to hug and call daddy. She watched him stand up and come over next to her, taking her spare hand.

"If you wouldn't mind opening one of your presents early, I think you may decide to wear your new gift." Lifting her to her feet, Dalton escorted his little girl into the living room and pointed to a stack of presents with her name. "The two boxes on top, open those and save the others for our Christmas together."

"You gave us all too many presents, Reverend Lane." She glanced down, the need to hug the loving, giving man, showing in her eyes. "I feel bad about the gift I made for you."

"You made me a gift?" Dalton lifted her face and saw the tears. He pulled her into a fatherly embrace, tears forming in his own eyes. "My beautiful Robin, any gift that you have made for me will be one of the most precious gifts I have ever received. I gave all of you, things you need, things you have wished for, but could not afford. It is what I want to do, sweet child, because your mother and all you beautiful children hold a special place in my heart and I truly love you."

Robin's arms looped around his waist tightly as her tears ran down her young face. She was taking that first step and soon, she thought, she would be able to call him daddy.

CHAPTER 24

"This is a lovely café, Ashley. Another little out-of-the-way spot and great for taking our time to talk about what is important in life." Bella looked over the impressive menu, then smiled up at the two staring faces. "Did I say something wrong? You're looking at me as though I have just stepped out of a wacky home." Bella laughed and placed the menu down to drink her water. "Well, tell me then, what is wrong with honest conversation between friends?"

"Why, nothing, I suppose." Ashley shook her confused head, then started reading the menu. "The today's special sounds wonderful, grilled salmon, house potatoes and Caesar salad with freshly crated cheese."

"I agree darling, I think that's what I'm having too." David smiled up at the server. "Could you bring us a bottle of your finest wine and the cheese dip with garlic bread sticks for an appetizer." He looked over at Bella as he took Ashley's hand "Ladies, are you ready to order?"

"I will have the Irish stew and since cheese is an option, you may melt a lovely amount on top." Bella past her menu to the server and sat back smiling.

"Very good dish, miss." His eyes fell on the couple "And you ma'am?"

"The gentleman and I will have todays special, dressing on the side." She retrieved David's menu and past it to the man as David added:

"And keep the bread sticks coming with our meal." He placed his napkin over his lap as the wine steward opened the bottle. "I trust this is a good year."

Bella couldn't help but laugh to herself as the wine steward pulled out the cork with a loud pop. Pouring a small amount for the doctor to taste, he said.

"This is an excellent wine sir, one of our most popular. It would appear from all the awards, that every year is a trademark year." The serious man waited for David to sample the wine and with a smile and a nod of approval, the steward smiled and poured out three glasses of wine before placing the bottle in a chilled wine bucket and walked stiffly through the kitchen door.

"Bella, my dear, what was funny about what David said to the wine steward?" Ashley could not find anything funny with the question, 'I trust this is a good year."

"I never meant to laugh at David's comment, but I have heard it many times before and some of the responses I remembered are very funny. Things like, 'Not particular, my wife left me for another man!' or 'Look pal, if you're not sure and it is already almost over, just try harder next year! or 'Trust can be tricky and I'm not seeing much different from last year! I wouldn't worry none, they're pretty much the same."

"I guess these people you heard…" Ashley tried to speak through her laughter. "They had no clue David was talking about the date the wine was made, some good years, some poor."

"You both learned a lot about wine when you toured Napa Valley a few years back, between your sister's pregnancies, didn't you?" Bella spooned out some dip in her small plate and nipped her breadstick in.

"That's right! Bella, I'm sure I never told you about our trip." Ashley glanced over at David who sipped on his wine as he watched Bella in fascination. Seeing Ashley questioning face, he shrugged his shoulders in confusion.

"Like I told you before my dear friend, how I know is not important. I can see plainly the love between you and yet you keep putting David in the background. Forgetting very important dates, like the dinner date with him. It wasn't just another date, was it David? You had planned to ask Ashley something very important, since it was your thirteenth anniversary."

"Oh, David, our thirteenth anniversary? It just slipped up on me, what with the movie deadline and all." Ashley could see the hurt return to David's eyes as he looked down. "Please David, forgive me." He remained quiet as Ashley reached for his hand that held her hand moments before. "David, please, say something."

"It wasn't just our anniversary you forgot, Ashley! You forgot our October dance under the stars, our long-time tradition since we told one another how we felt." David looked into her eyes "We told each other that we loved one another, that first night under the stars and hearing music from a distant live orchestra, we began dancing. It had become an October's romantic night, just for us, until you forgot and stood me up." Tears came into his eyes as he remembered standing there alone under the starlit canopy and hearing the orchestra playing their song. "It broke my heart Ashley and things just seem to get worse." David moved his hands for the food to be placed in front of him. "The day Bella called and asked me to come with you to Antler Knob, I had decided to call off our relationship and move where you could never find me. I was tired of being second in your life and thought maybe a different place, with time, I could forget I ever loved you."

"David, was I that cruel to you, my darling?" Ashley looked down as the server brought coffee and told them they could stay as long as they wanted, then walked away, leaving the pot. "What can I do to make up for all my mistakes?"

"I think what we need is to go back to the first time you two met." Bella put her elbows on the table and faced them. "As I recall David, you were not in the best of shape when Melinda Star stepped into your office thirteen years ago."

"I had just gotten out of a really bad relationship with a married woman. She was married to a wealthy businessman, conveniently for his money. He was a much older man and the young flirt hit on any available man that would fall for her charms, me included." David felt ashamed as he remembered those hotel meetings with the trashy redhead. "There was never any love involved in our relationship. It was just consensual sex and I realized I could lose my career, even my life if this bimbo's husband ever found out, so I broke it off. She threatened me for several months, then finally moved on, not wanting her husband to grow suspicious of her cheating lifestyle."

"So, during those months she threatened you, your life was turned upside down and you went to a so-call friend for help." Bella was glad they had stopped wondering how she knew their past or things that was going to happen. Her job was to bring two hearts together.

"I'm a doctor, for God's sake! I should have known the devastating effects drugs would have on me and I still became an attic!" David closed his eyes, knowing his past faults had to be told.

"David? I never suspected any misuse of drugs when I met you." Ashley wanted to cradle him in her arms until the pain of remembering went away.

"I had prepared my fix when my assistant knocked on my office door to inform me I had a very important patient waiting." David looked up into Ashley's eyes as he testified to what happened. "I stared at the needle, the need to feel the high that came within seconds of the shot, but Mrs. Clark, my angel of mercy, opened the door, walked over and took the needle from my hand and tossed it in my waste can. Taking my shoulders, she never scolded, but gave me wise counsel.

"David, I know you think this is helping take away all your misery, but believe me, the only thing it is accomplishing is digging you deeper into your despair and grief." With tears in her wise old eyes, she said "There is a chance to begin over David and your answer might lie just outside this door. Your new patient had to come in after hours because she didn't wish to be recognized by anyone. She is a very famous actress and her request for your help must be strictly confidential. After reading her paperwork and her reason for needing a great doctor, which you are sir, never in my entire career have I met anyone with so much love and compassion. But David, you cannot help this beautiful person in your current condition! Fire me if you are so inclined, sir, but I really care about you and the person you were before you fell into the spider's web." Then my wonderful assistant simply said "What's it going to be David? Death on drugs or life, fresh and a new beginning?"

"I walked away from my bad habit and into a new incredible life with you Ashley." David knew, without a doubt, that even if he was second in her life, after her acting career, he would never think of running away again. His place was with the woman he loved; his place was beside of Ashley.

"When I walked into the room and saw you sitting there looking at me with those alluring blue eyes, I could almost hear my heart beating in my chest, as if I was dreaming. Just moments before I had been shaking and sweating, needing a hit, but by some marvelous magic or miracle, all my need for the drug had simply vanished. It was not a star struck attraction that had me transfixed. To be honest, I didn't recognize you as Melinda Star right away. What I saw was a very sweet, nervous, and beautiful young lady who looked as though you were trying to decide in your mind if I was the right doctor for you. Perhaps you assumed I would have been an older man and my youth made you leery of my knowledge on so many degrees. I tried to put your worries away and prove that I was the right doctor to help you."

CHAPTER 25

"You are Doctor David Reynolds?" Ashley stood up to shake his hand. When the handsome young man walked inside the waiting room, Ashley had felt her heart leap. Never had she seen a more handsome man and suddenly the thoughts of telling him her reason for coming, felt embarrassing. "You look a lot younger than I had pictured, doctor. Your many degrees are very impressive. A transplant surgeon, heart specialist, and pediatrician, just to name a few."

"You have been doing your homework, Miss Andersen." Ashley had used her real name on the fill out sheet instead of her professional name to keep everything confidential. The one thing she didn't need was for the tabloids to get wind to what she was about to do.

"I need a doctor who can be totally discreet, Doctor Reynolds. In my line of work, a simple procedure can get the fox hounds hot on a celebrity's trail!" Ashley nervously sat back down, starting to feel anxious over her decision to pick a doctor from California. "In short, Doctor Reynolds, can I trust you to keep our patient-doctor procedure, a complete secret?"

"You have stoked my attention, Miss Andersen." Finally, after some time looking at her, David recognized the famous star without much make up. "Please tell me, Miss Star, what it is you wish done. Surely you are not requiring some kind of cosmetic surgery? You are already very attractive from head to toe."

"You have observed me very close then, Doctor Reynolds. I seek no cosmetic surgery of any kind and I will tell you in detail what it is I require from you sir, when I get your promise to hold tight to what I am about to ask you to do." Ashley sat back, waiting for his answer.

"Your secret will be safe with me, Miss Andersen." David walked around to the chair next to her and sat down. "My assistant is very professional as well and I trust her with my life."

Giving Hearts

"That is refreshing to know, Doctor Reynolds, but it is not your reputation that is at stake here." She had become very serious as she lend toward him. "Just one little leak could ruin my entire career. Can you appreciate that, doctor?"

"This is getting more and more intriguing Miss Andersen. Just what is it you want me to do?" David had never met anyone who brought out his inner self like this beautiful young woman and he was dying to know what it was she wanted done."

"I want to have a baby! My sister's baby!" she closed her eyes, glad to have it out. When she opened her eyes, the handsome doctor was staring into her eyes. "Well, you are a pediatrician, aren't you?"

"I am." David shook his head, amazed, never quite expecting that particular request. "So, you want to have a baby?"

"That's right! My sister's baby!" She was starting to grow aggravated.

"Why doesn't your sister have her own baby?" He couldn't help himself from smiling when she arched her eyebrow and growled.

"Look Doctor Reynolds, my sister would love to have her own baby if she possibly could, but she is uncapable of carrying a baby for nine months!" Ashley stood up, hands on hips "I am her twin sister and we are very close. She has always been there for me and now I can be there for her! The fertilized egg will belong to Allison and Joseph and you will implant it in me and be with me throughout the pregnancy. When it is due for delivery, you will fly with me to Antler Knob, North Carolina, where the baby must be born." Ashley walked nervously around the room while David watched her with interest. "My sister Allison will be in the delivery room with us and leave the private room with the baby. No one must know I had it. The only thing the people in that small town will know is Allison and Joseph Stevens just had a baby."

"Boy, you've got this all planned out, don't you Ashley Andersen?" David stood up and took hold of her shoulders. "Then would you explain what happens when Melinda Star starts showing?"

"Ha! Think you got me, doctor?" Ashley laughed "When I

see I cannot hide the baby any longer, I will take a little vacation. I have an understanding director and he is one of the only people I can rely on. Billy knows how important this is to me and believe me Doctor Reynolds, I will do it with or without your help."

"Yes, I believe you would Miss Andersen, but that isn't necessary. I will be more than happy to help you throughout your pregnancy." David sat back, his hands folded behind his head, enjoying her many different moods and actions. "Is there anything else I need to know before we get started?"

"You must always be ready to drop anything you are doing, with advanced noticed, of course, and go with me, especially when I will be making frequent visits to my sister. You must be her private doctor as well, seeing that the egg is removed at the appropriate time for fertilization.

Joseph will be on standby when you are ready for him." Ashley finally sat back down, glad the very talented doctor was taking her on. "When I start showing, I have a pregnancy prop, fake baby bump, for my sister to start wearing."

"One question, you said I needed to drop everything to go with you. Then you said, especially to visit your sister in Antler Knob, wherever that southern town is. Did you have somewhere else in mind for me to accompany you?" David smiled, trying to figure out this intriguing woman.

"Not exactly to accompany me, doctor, just come whenever I need your medical help." Ashley had mixed feelings about this man. For starters, she was afraid she might fall in love with him and she was far too busy making movies to get into a serious romance. But then, maybe, it was too late. These feelings were new to her and she was almost certain it was love at first sight. By his cool attitude and business manner, she never for once saw he was having the same feelings of love. The second feeling Ashley felt was total confidence in his skills. Not only a renowned pediatrician, but his scientific skills in the lab were known throughout the country.

"I would never dream of asking you to accompany me on my 'secret' vacation, Doctor Reynolds. It could be as long as three months."

"It might prove interesting, Miss Andersen. One way to get to know one another." Their eyes met for what seemed like a whole minute before Ashley glanced down, afraid her true feeling might show. She heard him chuckle softly, causing her to look up, cock her head in a defiant way, saying:

"I think we will learn all we need to know doctor about each other with my visits to your office."

Ashley stood up, slinging her bag over her arm. "I'm not looking for romance, Doctor Reynolds! I merely need a good reliable doctor who can take orders well and keep his mouth shut. If you have a problem with my rules, it's not too late to back out. But I must warn you, you will be passing up a large amount of money for doing the job."

"Oh, I won't be backing out of our arrangement, Miss Andersen. I will follow your rules and take your orders as long as I feel they are what's best for the baby, and you, of course." David Reynolds walked over to the door and hit a red button. "You can relax about me having any romantic intentions, Ashley Andersen. I am very capable of keeping this pregnancy strictly patient-doctor related and nothing more."

Having seen the red light come on, the signal from Doctor Reynolds that the meeting between him and his patient was over, Mrs. Doris Clark walked up smiling. David stepped back, out of the door and looked down at the beautiful woman, caught staring up at him.

"Mrs. Clark, would you make an appointment for Miss Andersen in two weeks. Be sure you have her sister's phone number so I can call her with a few personal questions."

"Personal questions?" Ashley arched her eyebrow. "I think I've told you everything you need to know!"

"Then, since you claim to know everything Miss Andersen, I take it you can tell me about your sister's female cycle." David couldn't help but chuckle when she turned a bright pink. "It something I have to know if I am going to be there to collect that little egg to fertilize."

"Very well doctor, call my sister then let me know when we need to travel to Antler Knob, a very unique small town in the mountains of North Carolina!" Ashley followed the friendly

Joan Byrd

assistant out the door and wrote down Allison's information for them, planning on giving her sister a call first from the doctor's front desk before leaving. After getting Mrs. Clarks permission to use the telephone, Ashley called Allison to warn her about the call she would be receiving from Doctor David Reynolds.

Leaving the building, Ashley took a breath of relief. Her plan was now set in motion and there would be no turning back. Allison's dream was to be the mother of a lot of children and now it was up to Ashley to make her dreams come true, just like her sister made sure she would have the acting career she had always dreamed about.

The one thing she had not planned on was falling in love with the doctor she would be spending five to six years around. He knew of only one baby, but to give Allison her complete dream, there would be more to follow. Ashley knew when the time was right, she would discuss the other pregnancies with David Reynolds, but for now, the beautiful, talented actress would take one day at a time.

CHAPTER 26

April was a beautiful month in North Carolina and although Antler Knob was cooler sitting on the mountain top, the first hardy spring flowers were popping up over the hills, in family gardens and the town flower pots that graced the sidewalks with seasonal plants and flowers. True to Ashley Andersen's description of Antler Knob, David Reynolds thought it was one of the warmest and most unique places he had ever seen. The old homes and family-owned businesses lined both sides of the narrow street where majestic white oaks grew on both sides, spaced perfectly apart. A single church steeple rose up high on the edge of town and it was obvious to the doctor, if you belonged to the church in town, you had to be a Methodist.

Ashley and her doctor were to meet up with Allison and Joseph at the Angel of Mercy Clinic, located near the children's home where the twins grew up. Doctor Reynolds had arranged with the local resident doctor that he needed access to both a lab and a patient's examining room. Privacy was utmost important to both doctor and patient. Doctor Reynolds had assured Doctor Marvin Lewis, Allison's old doctor, that her case was serious and he was up on all the latest techniques in a difficult pregnancy. Marvin Lewis had agreed to release all her papers, somewhat relieved over this younger doctor taking over at Ashley Andersen, Allison's twin sister, request.

David first met with the two sisters and collected several healthy-looking eggs to choose from, and earlier he had sent Joseph Stevens inside another room to collect his specimen so he conducted the process of fertilization. Stepping out into the hallway expecting to find it empty, David immediately noticed Joseph Stevens casually reading a book. Allison's husband smiled up at the surprised doctor.

"I know what you're thinking doc. How on earth did I get it done so quickly?" Joseph laughed at his statement. "Doc, the truth is, I cannot give you a specimen. I was told I was sterile because of my lifelong fight with drugs, which started inside my mother's womb. I'm also infected with a rare blood disease that kept me from being a flyer pilot in the Air Force and now...," tears swelled up in his brown eyes. "I cannot give my darling Allison what she wants most in this world, babies."

"Then why did you waste all of our time, Mr. Stevens and why did you give your wife and her sister Ashley false hopes with having this baby you cannot deliver?" David Reynolds had never hit another man before but he had to fight the notion for striking this man in the face. "No specimen, no fertilization, no baby!"

"Oh, I'm sorry if I mislead you doc just now, but there will be a sample for you just as soon as my friend has collected it." Joseph chuckled, remembering how nervous Dalton had been over the process.

Dalton Lane had paced the floor, thinking if he didn't get turned on pretty soon, Allison would catch him leaving the stimulating room and his promise to Joseph to keep his contribution a secret would be out in the open. Dalton stopped in front of a mirror and stared at his reflection. He was a minister, a man of God and he knew if he thought for one minute about the one he truly loved, his Allison and got turned on, he would be committing a sin as the words kept floating through his mind, over and over. 'If you only look at another man's wife with lust in your heart, you have committed adultery.'

"I cannot hurt my God! I cannot let my friend down either! And, how would I ever live with myself if I was the one responsible for Allison to never have children." Dalton got on his knees to speak to God. "I truly know all Your teachings are just and right and I live my life trying to follow your word and do that which is right in Your sight. I know what sacrifice you made for all your friends when you laid your life down. Now, my friend is dying and this is his only request to me: be the father to his children! Is this not a little bit like laying down my life for my friend so he can leave this world with the peace of mind that he kept his promise to the girl he has always loved? It's true that I love the same beautiful girl, but you know I loved her way before I knew Joseph cared for her. I can see now that

Allison truly loved me and only married my friend when she thought I didn't feel that way about her, but she is and has always been the love of my life. I hurt her one time by letting her go, but I will not hurt the one I love by destroying her dreams of becoming a mother. Forgive me, but it is the only way for me to give that which I have. Without her, I am only half alive, but maybe, if I can dream she still belongs to me, if for a short while, I can give her the hope to live on."

So, Dalton Lane drew himself into a world with Allison and only with his thoughts of having her in his arms, to hold, to kiss, and to finally make love to. The minister had his specimen ready for Doctor Reynolds when he knocked on the door and met a new friend, he would come to know over the next few years.

Time Goes Back to Bella, Ashley and David

"So, Ashley, you now carried your sister's baby and you never guessed the baby's father wasn't Joseph." Bella followed the couple as they found a quiet bench out of the wind, directly in the bright sunshine. "A warm spot to sat on such a cold winter's day." Bella smiled upward. "The Lord provides what His children need."

"He certainly does, Bella." David pulled Ashley in closer to help keep her warm. "I never knew Dalton was a minister until the second baby needed a specimen. When I gave him the cup and the test tube to pour it in, he told me he hoped it would be easier this go-round. Dalton then filled me in on the reasons he couldn't get turned on and I could sympathies with his reasoning."

"Never-the-less the good reverend helped contribute to Allison and Joseph's family tree and it's obvious he is attached to all five children, as well as their mother." Bella never felt the cold like ordinary people, so she happily breathed in the cold fresh air. "Ashley, you tried to keep your distance from David for as long as you could, but then, around the end of September you began to show."

"It was slow at first and all I could think about was completing the film. Two more scenes and I could disappear for three months, have the baby, then start the next film, while preparing to get pregnant again, spacing the children two years apart." Ashley laid her head over on David shoulder, feeling loved and safe as she recalled what happened. "David had set up a visit to Antler Knob two weeks before Christmas. The baby was to be born sometime in between those two weeks. I had called Allison, telling her to start wearing the first baby bump, then gradually progress to the last one around the eighth month. She said it was almost comical that no one guessed the truth and her friends even gave her two baby showers." Ashley then sat up smiling, remembering the day David showed up at her vacation home she had bought in New York City.

"Doctor Reynolds, is something wrong?" I tried to sound businesslike, but I had never been happier to see anyone like I was him in my entire life. I wanted to pull him inside the door, then loop my arms around his neck and feel his lips on mine. He stood, staring down into my eyes for what seemed like an eternity, then he swept me up in a warm embrace as his lips parted over mine in a passionate kiss. Then he pulled away and turned, with the intention of leaving when I stopped him.

"Doctor Reynolds, do you just intend to sweep me into your arms, kiss me as though you care, then simply smile and walk away?" I wanted desperately for him to stay, to never leave my side again, but how could I confess such love and devotion to a man I could not read. Did David love me or was he only playing games with me? A quickly growing fat movie star about to have a baby?"

"Ashley, ask me the right way, and I might believe this thing I know we both feel can grow and become alive." David had stopped and turned to look at me seriously as he added. "If you had any doubts before about how you feel about me, after that kiss, you should know the truth. What's it to be Miss Andersen? Do I walk out that door and meet you in Antler Knob, just as your doctor, or do I stay, and be the man in your life, who will love you forever?"

"I know I said I never wanted anything romantic between us, but I was really fighting my true feelings for you." Ashley reached for his hand and gently pulled him through the door as he shut it slowly with his foot. "I want you in my life to David." She stopped talking when she heard music just outside her balcony. It sounded like a big orchestra from the sound stage across the street. David had heard it too and led her outside on the balcony. It was a starlet night, and there was a romantic moon shining over head as David swept her in his arms and spoke very softly.

"May I have this dance with the woman I love?"

"It will be a pleasure dancing with the man I love under the stars." Then they began to play what became 'our song' "Till There Was You" and after that night, every October 20th became our anniversary to meet in New York at my house and dance on the balcony under the stars, after paying an orchestra to play our song across the street."

And back on the cold bench, David once again recalled the last anniversary he stood on that balcony alone, looking up at the stars with tears filling his eyes as the orchestra played "Till There Was You" And how the thought of being stood up on their very special night still reeling in his head, then Ashley forgetting their romantic dinner date, where he had planned to ask her to be his wife. David had gotten to the point of despair and wanted to call it quits, this time for good. The first time he had grown weary of her neglecting him, they had a bad argument over her choosing her film career over their living together. The five babies had been born and he felt as if she had no more use for him. Just as he was packing up to leave town, Ashley showed up at his apartment in tears, begging for another chance. She had heard their song and all those beautiful memories came back and over ruled her career. She promised David she would never put him last again, and she was true to her word, at least until the big break she had been waiting for came. Billy had called with the good news she had landed the main role of Helena, with Robert Redford and Gene Hackman. Promising David that he would have the best of her, they remained happy for only a short time, until all her old habits started creeping back in, little by little. First, it was the little things Ashley would forget, but when it came to the things that made them the happiest and she forgot about them, things deteriorated quickly and David was ready to give up on their relationship.

"Sometimes we lose track of what is really important in our life, Ashley." Bella reached for her hand. "David gave up all

Joan Byrd

his patients just to give you his full attention when you wanted to have your sister's babies for her. He never did it for the large amount of money you paid him. David was wealthy already from a large inheritance from his parents and from the money he required from his practice. He would have done it for free just to be by your side whenever he could. It was obvious you loved David just as deeply, but your dream of becoming that famous movie star had never burned out and because of it, you kept your eyes closed in that dream world until you almost lost what mattered most. Your love for David and a lifetime of happiness with him. Ashley, you dropped everything for your sister when you learned she needed a new kidney and flew here, not caring when that film might be finished. You found the love for your sister was more important than your career. The same respect should be given to David, who has loved you the moment he saw you. Not as Melinda Star, but as Ashley Andersen, the same sweet girl who grew up right here over thirty years ago."

"Bella is right David. I have been a selfish actress, always putting my dream first, or at least it was the dream of a five-year-old orphan." Ashley touched David's face, as though she were seeing the man she loved for the first time, all over again. "I have a new dream now David. A dream that is filled with everlasting love with the man I want to spend the rest of my life with. If I ever make any more movies, it will be on your terms, my darling. And I promise as soon as this film is complete, I am going to take off one whole year to devote to our wedding and long honeymoon!"

"Ashley, my dearest Ashley! I have waited so long to hear you commit your life to me and to do it right here in Antler Knob, right before Christmas." David pulled her up and fell on his knee as he pulled a small box from his pocket. "An early Christmas present my love. Will you marry me, Ashley Andersen?"

Ashley smiled through tears at the sparkling diamond in his hand and shaking her head happily said "Yes, yes, yes!"

Bella watched and smiled as she looked upward and whispered "One more Christmas Eve miracle! Now to win the big contest and make it another miracle on Christmas Eve!"

CHAPTER 27

December the 23rd came in cloudy, with a good chance of snow, but to twelve-year-old Robin Stevens it only meant that Christmas in Antler Knob would be even more crowded with visitors who loved the holiday spirit of the small town. She was excited for three reasons. The first was Mandy Montgomery's birthday party, sure to be filled with games and great prizes for whoever won. The ones attending would be all of Mandy's rich neighbors and other rich school friends, making Robin the exception. She wasn't exactly poor, but since her mother had gotten ill, the family had to watch what they spent and most of their money went for the daily essentials like food, heat, the power bill, phone bill, water bill and doctor bills, just to name a few.

When Robin had opened her Christmas gift from Dalton Lane, she had fought back the tears that swelled up in her eyes. Looking at herself in the mirror, Robin felt like a real Christmas princess in her red dress and red shoes to match. Tucked away in the dress box was a smaller box than contained a wreath neckless with matching earrings. Now, she thought, I will blend in with the other girls, not that it really bothered her that she was different. Mandy loved her for being Robin and their close friendship had proved to be a solid bond.

Reverend Lane had promised to come by and take her to the party at Mandy's then return for her, so she could change for the dress rehearsal, which was the second thing that had the young girl excited.

Robin had learned that the big movie director had come to Antler Knob with a big truck filled with Hollywood props and costumes, just for the church group. Her mother had taken her to see the Saturday evening classic movies, all of them Christmas holiday movies as a birthday present since she, like her friend Mandy was born close to Christmas, Robin's being Christmas Eve. The movie "White Christmas" had been one of her favorites. The mountain ski slopes and the hope for snow reminded Robin of Antler Knob. The costumes, fabulous Christmas tree, the horse and sleigh making its way around the drive, when Mr. Crosby opened the big barn-like door behind the stage and snow finally falling. It was made even more magical to such a young girl. Then there was the singing and dancing, same as her group would be doing on at least half the stage at the Antler Knob Theater.

Robin smiled when she remembered Ronnie, the choir director, grab Reverend Lane on the way in the church at the last rehearsal, panicking over their lead singer, Robert Brandon getting laryngitis and demanding the preacher take his place singing the lead or he was going to throw up his hands and quit. Without a second thought, Dalton agreed to sing, and Robin could not believe her ears at his beautiful baritone voice as he began singing O Holy Night, which brought her to the third thing that had her so intense.

Robin was so sure that Dalton Lane was her biological father that she had carved out a small trophy, shaped like the Methodist symbol, the cross and the flame. Getting a little bit of her mama's painting skills, she had carefully painted it and with a steady hand printed, TO MY FATHER, DALTON LANE, I LOVE YOU DADDY! ROBIN!

Robin didn't just come up with the answer from her strong resemblance to the handsome minister. She was the only Steven child with raven black hair and emerald-green eyes, same as Reverend Lane. Taylor, Tyler, Jonathan, and Hannah all had blonde hair and blue eyes like their beautiful mother, Allison. Not one Steven child had brown hair and brown eyes like their daddy, Joseph Stevens. Robin walked to her window and looked out at the first flakes of snow falling and let her mind drift back to a similar day when she became eight.

Joseph had watched his oldest child staring at her reflection in the different mirrors throughout the house. At times, he noticed, she would be holding a family portrait, first looking tensely at the picture, then at herself in the mirror. As she laid down her mother's hand mirror, Joseph lovingly took her small hand and led her to his office, so they could talk in privacy.

Joseph loved all five of his children with Allison, and he could tell his Robin was confused about her appearance, noticing their differences.

"Baby girl, I have noticed you've been looking at yourself a lot lately. Is it because you are our only child that has black hair?"

"Yes daddy." Robin looked up at him, questions written on her sweet innocent face. "My eyes are a different color too, daddy. My two sisters and two brothers have hair and eyes like mama, my yellow crayon and my blue crayon. My hair is like my black crayon and my eyes are like my green crayon. You've got just two brown crayons, daddy." Tears filled her emerald-green eyes. "Daddy, why am I different? Mr. Collins ask you if I belonged to the milk man. Do I daddy?"

"Mr. Collins was just saying a bad joke, sweetheart." Joseph pulled her up onto his lap. "You are truly our little girl, Robin. Your mama had you eight years ago on Christmas Eve. It was truly the best Christmas present your mama and I ever received." Joseph knew he could never tell a small child of eight the truth, so he would opt for a little white lie instead. "The reason your hair is as raven as the night and your eyes are as green as an emerald is simple to explain. My beautiful grandmother was born Irish-American Indian and old photos my mother had, showed her dark black hair, after the Indians and her emerald green eyes after her Irish ancestress. Do you understand what I am saying?"

"I think so daddy. I look like your Irish-Indian grandmother?" Robin wondered what the woman looked like and wished her daddy's mama had given him a picture of her mama.

But of course, Joseph had no real way of knowing what either of his grandmothers looked like and the sad truth was, Joseph didn't even remember what his mother looked like, his father either, for that matter. How could he remember anything from those nightmare days living with abusive parents, a very tiny child living in constant pain from the beatings and the drug effects. So, Joseph had to tell his loving child about make-believe parents, a mama and daddy who loved him, hugged him and cared for his needs, just like he vowed he would always do for his children.

"It's been a long time since I saw my loving grandmother's picture sweetheart, but I could never forget that beautiful black hair and could only imagine her green eyes. The portraits were in black and white, but the colors came to life when mama described her." Joseph set her down before standing up. Oh, how he would have loved to have lifted her up into his once strong arms, but his sickness had grown worse and he knew he only had a few months to live. This is one thing he would keep from all his babies until he had to say his goodbyes.

He felt Robin's small hand take his and he looked down into her smiling face. This, he thought, would be another memory snapshot he would take with his head and store in his heart, then carry all of them with him to Heaven when he left his five kids and his Allison.

"Thank you for telling me about your grandmother." Her little hand squeezed his as she added "I love you daddy! I'm real glad I'm your little girl!"

Robin looked out at the snow, coming down harder, but it was hard to see it from all the tears that filled those emerald-green eyes. She gazed upward and whispered:

"I miss you so much, Daddy! Please don't be mad at me for giving your best friend that trophy I carved out. I know the truth now, daddy. I'm sorry but I needed to know and went to mama and ask her about my grandmother with black hair and emerald-green eyes, your grandmother." The young girl lifted a tissue from her box to wipe her eyes, as the tears continued to fall. "She told me about your real parents, daddy. How they beat you and threw you out in the rain, hoping you were dead." Another Kleenex, then another, before she could speak to the man she had loved with all her heart for eight short years. "Mama said there was no way you could have known anything about your grandmother, being so young, but she asked me to never hold that against you. Mama said you had seen me hurting, thinking I wasn't really your or mama's baby girl and confused by what Mr. Collins had said. Mama said Max Collins never thought before he spoke and he could say some pretty hurtful things. I realized later Mama was absolutely right about Max Collins when I heard him ask you at the grocery store, "Dang Joseph, just how much longer are you going to be with us?" and I thought he was referring to our being in the grocery store too long. I never thought then the rude man was talking about you…dying." More tissues wiped away fresh tears as she sniffed. "Mama told me not to worry about my beautiful black hair and special green eyes. She said I was honestly and truly your little girl and the photo of her carrying me from the hospital was more than enough proof that she was my mother. But back to the gift I made Reverend Lane.

I have watched the way mama and our minister look at one another, how Dalton has always been here for anything we need, especially mama. Then I began putting little things together. If we sit side by side in a photo and the photographer did not know us, he would surely say, this is going to be a wonderful father and daughter picture. We look that much alike, but no one else ever seems to notice the strong resemblance, but me.

I've waited in Reverend Lane's office on several occasions for him to take me home and noticed all the great carvings lining his shelfs. He saw me looking at them and asked if I was interested in what they were? Since I had been dibbling in a few carved pieces at home, I was very intrigued by all the life-like birds, squirrels, and rabbits." Robin looked up and smiled as she remembered the minister showing her his beautiful collection. "Reverend Lane told me he had carved every one of those birds and critters, as he put it, when he lost his girlfriend to another man and needed something to take his mind off of her." Robin walked away from the window and picked up the carved robin, given to her that day by Dalton Lane. "So, that is the second thing we have in common daddy, we both enjoy carving." She set the robin back beside her two carved birds, a blue bird and a cardinal, almost as good as the preacher's.

"I found out Reverend Lane can write, just like me. He has written a sacred song for the concert tomorrow night and I wrote a cheerful little song to add to our first group of numbers. I have been asked by our choir director to sing it as a solo, with the choir coming in with harmony on the chorus. I am really happy it turned out so good, just like it sounded in my head when I wrote it. I'm sure you remember how much I've always loved to sing and started with the children's choir at five years old and now daddy, I am singing with the adult choir, at twelve. Mama said you would be so proud of me. You know what daddy, I think you are proud of me, smiling down from Heaven." Robin had checked the bedside clock and hurried to wash her face and recomb her long dark hair. As she prepared for Dalton to pick her up, she smiled upward.

"Daddy, forgive me, but I have heard you try to sing, just like mama, and I have to admit, neither one of you can carry a tune, although you both tried and made a joyful 'noise' unto the Lord, at church. Which leads me to the other reason I believe your best friend is my blood father. Never have I heard a more beautiful voice than when Reverend Lane started singing "O Holy Night" at practice yesterday. He could have easily become a professional singer. But I still wasn't 100% sure until Clara, she's a wonderful lady who has come into our life and made us have hope again, well, Clara saw me contemplating all the similarities between me and Reverend Lane and approached me, feeling my struggles. I was so happy she had taken notice and, like an angel, flew to my side to help.

CHAPTER 28

"Miss Robin, you look like you are trying to solve the mystery of Antler Knob and even with all your good clues, you are still baffled." Clara always knew how to cheer a person up, starting with a steaming cup of hot chocolate, topped with a mound of melting marsh mellows. "Just sip on this a while and let's see if we can clear up the case of matching identity and exact personalities and talents."

No one could understand how Clara knew so much about us. Our past, our presence and our future, but, for some unknown reason, she knew, and had the art of telling us. It wasn't just the fact she had witness for herself how much Reverend Lane and I looked alike or had the same talent for writing and singing. Those were obvious things any ordinary person should have noticed, but it was a lot of little things she knew, that I hadn't told anyone about, including my mama. Then she same as said the very same thing I had been thinking moments before while waiting for her to speak.

"Robin, sweet girl, you are absolutely right! To anyone who has good vision, it is obvious you look exactly like Dalton Lane. And even the dumbest person in the room, much like Max Collins, can place your talents for writing and singing together." Clara chuckled "But I bet I'd be safe to bet, no one knows about a certain wooden gift, carved in the shape of a robin, was given to one Robin Stevens by her dear friend Reverend Lane. Neither would they know the blue bird and the red cardinal, sitting on either side of your robin was carved by, none other than Miss Robin Stevens herself. Am I warm to hot on the truth, sweet child?" Clara reached over to pat her dark locks.

"I've never told a single soul about that gift, Clara." Robin remembered how sad Reverend Lane had looked when he spoke about losing his girlfriend to another man. "I could tell he must have loved that woman with all his heart and that was probably the reason he had never married."

"Now, now, sweet girl. There was one person you told. Maybe, you just forgot because you were only six." Clara remembered back to the Sunday when the children had to stay and rehearse their Christmas play to be presented the following Sunday. "Dalton had told your parents that he would see that you got home after practice because the twins had come down with a bad cough and the dark clouds had brought in a new coat of snow to Antler Knob and they didn't want to expose their sick children to the elements outside, afraid it might turn to pneumonia."

Years Earlier

"Robin, you did great in the roll of Mary." Mrs. Stallings, her Sunday school teacher had walked her down the hall to the preacher's study. "Now darling, just find you a seat and wait in here. Reverend Lane will be back in just a few minutes. I will be right down the hall, seeing the other children off with Miss Myers."

"Yes ma'am, I'll wait here." Robin sat, kicking her feet back and forth in the adult chair as she scanned the tall bookcases filled with all sorts of things. Books, neatly arranged by height, A large frame picture of Jesus, smiling with a group of children. Robin smiled and jumped down from the high seat as she walked over to study the face of Jesus. She smiled, then noticed all the colorful wooden birds on one entire shelf. Looking around to make sure no one was watching, she managed to push the chair over in front of the birds. She needed to see them up close, so she crawled up in the chair, then stood, her young eyes as wide as her bright smile.

Reverend Lane walked in and his first concern was for the child's safety as he quickly made his way to her side. Startled by his actions, Robin quickly jumped down and stared at the floor, afraid of a spanking.

"Robin, what are doing climbing on such a tall chair? You could have fallen and I am supposed to be watching after you." Reaching down, Dalton gently lifted her chin "Don't be afraid sweet child, I could never harm you. You are Allison's little girl."

120

"I'm really sorry if I scared you, Reverend Lane." Robin blinked her big green eyes. "I'm really used to climbing on things. Me and Tater, he's my friend who lives next door, we climb trees and his swinging bars."

"Tater?" Dalton raised his eyebrow and smiled. "Is that your friend's real name? Tater?"

Robin giggled "Oh, no sir! That's just what I call him! His name is Tommy and he calls me mater." Another giggle.

"I see! Tater and Mater, the six-year-old tree and swinging bar climbers!" Again, the preacher chuckled as he lifted Robin back on the chair, feeling more in charge if she started slipping he was there to catch her. "What is it up here you like, Robin?"

"I really like all those colorful birds!" Her young eyes fell on the squirrels and rabbits. "Golly gee, Reverend Lane, those little rabbits look just like they might hop right off the shelf and that looks just like the squirrel me and Tater chased up the big oak tree in our back yard."

"I'm glad you like all my critters." He enjoyed watching the excitement on her face as she studied each carved figure and finally said.

"Reverend Lane, where did you get all these pretty critters?" Robin had said it so seriously Dalton tried to snaffle his laugh.

"I made them, some years ago, when I was feeling really sad and needed something to take my mind off my troubles."

Robin reached over and placed her small hand on his handsome face, her young face showing pity as she said softly, "Why was you sad Reverend Lane? I don't want you to be sad."

"What a precious child you are, Robin Stevens." Dalton had felt like hugging the sweet little girl, but instead he told her the reason for his sadness. "I was once in love with the most beautiful, most incredible young lady I have ever met. I wanted to marry her more than anything I've ever wanted and start a family. I know she was in love with me too, but things happened and I lost my girlfriend to another man." Dalton knew it was foolish telling such a young child about the love he had and still had for her mother, although he would not tell her that part. Just what little ears might understand. "So, to help me forget, I started carving all these critters, then I painted them, so they could come alive."

"Come alive?" Robin's eyes grew wide as she looked back at the figures, wondering if they would start to move.

"Not really alive, just make them so realistic, you can almost see the rabbits hop or wiggle their nose, sniffing for grass. The squirrel's scurrying up at tree or burying a big fat acorn. See the birds flutter their wings and let out a chirp, then it turns into a song." Dalton patted her long pigtails and noticed the tears in her green eyes.

"Reverend Lane, is that why you never got married? Do you still want to marry your beautiful and incredible girlfriend and have a family?"

Dalton was amazed that she had understood all his words and as he lifted her down from the chair, he simply said, "If it's meant for us to be together someday, we will." And that was exactly how he felt as he helped the small child in her coat then reached for his. He noticed she looked back up toward the robin sitting on the end of the shelf. Not needing a chair to reach the bird, he took it down carefully and pulled some tissue from his desk drawer to wrap it up, then he handed the gift to Robin. "This is a gift to my young friend Robin, from your minister and friend. Place it someplace safe in your room and imagine it singing you awake in the mornings."

"Oh, thank you! My very own critter. I'll put it beside the one I carved." She smiled at his surprised face. "It took me a long time, because I was really careful with daddy's knife, then I borrowed mama's paints and brushes. It turned out pretty, but not as pretty as this one."

"Maybe when you get a little older and its safer to use your daddy's knife." Dalton grabbed his car keys and her hand and in a fatherly manner said, "If you promise to put your daddy's knife back where you found it and return your mama's things to her, I will help you with your carvings and get you some wood that carves the figures out easier." She nodded and smiled as he helped her in the car. "Will you promise? I just don't want you to hurt yourself Robin. Knives can be very dangerous and little children should never play with them. Do you understand? If anything happened to you, your mama would never forgive herself. She would cry her heart out."

"I told Reverend Lane I would take daddy's knife back and wait until I was old enough to use it. He seemed to be relaxed and happy again as we drove home." Robin looked up at the caring woman "You know Clara, now that I think of it, Reverend Lane never one time mentioned my daddy being worried or that I was Joseph's little girl, like he had mama."

"And maybe that is why you told your daddy about the bird Reverend Lane gave you?" Clara refreshed the young girl's memory. "Remember? It was after the good reverend brought you home and your daddy was tucking you in for the night. He had asked you how the practice went and why you were a little late getting home."

CHAPTER 29

"Let's get you all tuck in, baby girl." Joseph pulled Robin's covers up and sat down on the side of her bed, letting his hand gently hub her head. "How did practice go? Did you get a solo?"

"Practice went very well daddy!" Robin gave him a sweet smile. "My teacher asked me to sing 'Away in a Manger' cause I'm Mary!"

"Mary? Well now, that's about the most important role in any Christmas play, with the exception the baby Jesus, which is usually a doll, or some towels wrapped up in a pretty little blanket." Joseph loved to see his daughter happy about using her talents. She had been singing like an angel ever since she could talk, and he knew she didn't get that gift from him or Allison. "Who is Joseph this year?"

"Johnny Brandon, but he isn't singing a solo." Robin giggled remembering the six-year-old telling their teacher that he could act but he didn't want to sing. "Johnny said only mommies sing lullabies, not daddies." Joseph laughed, along with his daughter, then asked:

"Sweetheart, why were you and Reverend Lane a little late getting home tonight? Your mama and I were starting to worry about you."

"We just lost tract of time daddy. Reverend Lane was showing me all his critters!" she giggled, remembering all the realistic carvings.

"Critters? Dalton has critters in his church study?" Joseph sat up, unsure of what to think.

"Reverend Lane has one whole shelf lined up with birds, rabbits and squirrels! I asked him where he got them all and he told me he had made them. He said he made them some years ago when he was feeling really sad and needed something to take his mind off his troubles."

"Some years ago? Did Dalton tell you why he was so sad he needed to keep that busy?" Joseph thought it unusual for his friend to share his past with his daughter, but if there was one thing Joseph knew, he knew he could trust Dalton Lane and his judgements.

"He did daddy, 'cause I asked him why was he so sad. Then I told him I didn't want him to be sad. Reverend Lane is a special man daddy and I really like him a lot." Remembering her friend's sadness showing in his eyes, brought real tears to her young eyes.

"Sweetheart, did Reverend Lane say anything when you told him you didn't want him to be sad?" Joseph knew his friend had been hiding something from him and he knew somehow Allison was involved.

"He said I was a precious child, Daddy, and I think that's why he told me what made him sad."

"You know Dalton is my very best friend, baby girl, so I would love to know what made him that sad." Joseph wanted to know everything and his time was running out. "Can you remember what he told you?"

"Sure daddy, just like I can remember my bedtime stories that you or mama tell me." Robin sit up and smiled at her gift from Dalton before speaking. "Reverend Lane said he once was in love with the most beautiful and incredible young lady he had ever met. He wanted to marry her more than anything he ever wanted and start a family. He said he knew she was in love with him too, but things happened and I lost my girlfriend to another man."

"Another man?" Joseph couldn't help but believe that other man was himself. "I think I'll ask Dalton to show me those critters after the holidays. Maybe he put a date somewhere on them and I can figure out just who the lucky woman is that stole my best friend's heart."

"You don't need to see all those critters daddy if mine has a date on it somewhere." Robin smiled when her father asked, "Yours? He gave you one of those...critters?"

"Up there, Daddy, next to my blue bird!" Robin pointed out the brown bird with the orange breast. "It's a robin, just like my name." She watched her daddy lift it off the shelf and turn it over. "Isn't it beautiful, Daddy? Does it have a date on the bottom?"

Robin noticed the tears falling down her father's face, so she pulled her covers back and climbed out of bed, then walked to his side. "What's wrong daddy? Why are you crying?"

"Daddy is just feeling a little sad for his old pal, baby girl, that's all." Joseph had seen the date and the truth poured into his soul like a lightning bolt, knowing who the beautiful and incredible young lady was and who had taken her from him. Dalton must have found out about his health report somehow from the Air Force entry department. Joseph had never found out the truth about his rare blood disease until the exam to see if he could have children, since Allison couldn't have a healthy baby and lost their only little baby even before it started to grow. Dalton had willingly given up his happiness so his best friend could finally find true happiness and... Joseph remembered the words he had spoken to Dalton after telling him all about his Ali. "He knew I was dying when I told him if I could make Ali my wife, I would be the happiest man alive and I would be happy...as long as I...lived." He thought as he felt his daughter tug at his pajama sleeve. "You need to get back in bed, baby girl." Joseph placed the carved robin back on the shelf and taking his daughter's hand, walked her back to the bed and helped her in, then covered her back up. "Don't look so sad, Robin, daddy is just tired and I need to still check on Taylor and Tyler and see if the medicine has taken down their fever."

"I'm sure they'll get all better, daddy." Robin gave him a sweet kiss and a tight hug. "I'll ask Jesus to make them all better, tonight when I pray."

"My friend Dalton was right Robin Marie Stevens, you are one precious little girl and daddy loves you with all his heart." Joseph kissed her forehead and clicked out her bed lamp. "Now, say your prayers and close those beautiful green eyes. Goodnight sweetheart."

"Goodnight daddy." Then she remembered one more thing from the conversation with her minister friend. "Oh, daddy!" he turned and smiled. "I did ask Reverend Lane, was the reason he had never married, because he still wanted to marry his beautiful, incredible girlfriend and have a family. You know what he said?"

"What did my friend say?" Joseph closed his eyes in the dark, needing to know but afraid of what he might hear.

"Reverend Lane said, if it is meant to be for us to be together someday, we will." Robin scooted under the sheets and closed her eyes to pray as Joseph Stevens slipped out the door and stood frozen in the hallway.

"Surely my friend is not waiting for me to die and…" Joseph began to weep, recalling how Dalton had always helped him and given him unconditional love, never wanting nothing in return. Joseph knew his friend would have laid down his life for him and in a sense, he did. The day he chose to let Joseph be the one to have happiness with Allison, the one beautiful, incredible girl who stole his heart and still has it. He had sensed their strong love for one another for a long time, although neither one had ever openly shown it. Allison was the perfect wife, loyal and faithful. Dalton was the perfect friend, also loyal and faithful and both of them had given him the most perfect love a wife or a best friend could give.

Now Joseph knew Dalton gave his all, all his future happiness, his future family and all the joys and love that goes with it. "No!" Joseph thought "Dalton is not waiting for his best friend to die. Instead, if it were possible, I know he would take my place and let me live on, loving and caring for his girl, his…children." Joseph picked up a picture of his very best friend "Because of you Dalton, I have lived to be the happiest man in the world and when it is my time to depart this life, it will be time for your life to begin and be the happiest man in the world! You gave me your dearest love! You gave it with all your heart and soon, I will give her back into the rightful arms of the man she has always loved!"

"And now that you know, dear friend, I want you to know, I do not wish or pray for your departure." Dalton had stayed behind to make sure little Robin replaced the sharp knife and had heard Joseph pouring out his heart. Joseph turned to see his friend also had tears streaming down his face. "I pray that you could live to become an old man, along with Allison and me, still tagging along. We could go fishing on some golden pond, liked we always talked about when we found ourselves in the ditch on Saturdays as youth at the orphanage."

"Or returning to our 60th class reunion and find a room filled with old men and women, and we would swear we hadn't changed a bit." Joseph laughed as he remembered making that comment when they both graduated Reynolds High School.

"And we both would be excited to see the most popular girl in school, Tracy Hunter, red hair, down to her shapely hips, and that little twist when she walked that made all the boys whistle." Dalton chuckled, thinking about his remarks. "She would probably be fat, grey hair, piled up in a tight bun, wearing black rim glasses, but...she would still have that twist to turn all us old men on!"

"I hate to miss all the old classmates, but where I'll be going, I will be forever young and no one from our class will have a chance to laugh at me again." Joseph hugged his friend. "Dalton, I have no clue why you are still here pal, but I'm glad you stayed."

"Me too, but I'm not ready to say goodbye yet pal so just hang on for as long as you can." Dalton held on tight, knowing Joseph was told he only had three to four more years. "I need you, Allison needs you, and your children need you."

"Thank you, Dalton, for everything!" Joseph took a deep breath as he stepped back and smiled.

"Seriously, I still don't know why you are still here. I thought we said goodbye at the door one hour ago."

"And we did, but I had some unfinished business here I needed to witnessed being done." Dalton knew his friend was totally confused when he heard noise coming from Robin's room. He pulled Joseph in the shadows as the little girl slipped from her room and made her way quietly down the dimly lit hall, into Joseph's office. They followed at a safe distance and watched as she pulled something from her robe, wrapped in a newspaper, then carefully unwrap it and put it back inside the middle drawer of her daddy's desk. Quickly, the two men jumped behind the door as she went to the small room where Allison did her painting and replace her mother's paint and brushes before running quickly back to her room. Joseph stared up at his best friend.

"Dalton, what just happened there?"

"Your precious little girl has taken up wood carving, and that was long before she saw my collection." Dalton smiled, remembering her fascination over his carvings. "Robin told me she would put the bird I gave her next to the one she had carved. After asking her about it, she said she had borrowed her daddy's knife to carve out the blue bird, then borrowed her mama's paint and brushes to color it with."

"My little girl has been using my sharp knife? Carving wood?" Joseph sank in his desk chair, suddenly nervous about leaving it were any of his children could get a hold of it. "Dang Dalton! My little girl could have cut herself bad, even killed herself and it would have been my stupid fault! What kind of father am I?"

"You are a wonderful father, my friend. Your children know to keep out of your room, especially, to stay away from dangerous weapons." Dalton tried to reassure his friend "I know what you're thinking my friend. You are wondering why then did your very smart little girl sneak inside her daddies' desk drawer and borrow his bowie knife."

"Yes, I am. Her mother and I have worn her, along with all our children, the dangers that come from playing with knives and guns." Joseph pulled off his keychain and locked the drawer. "I guess children just don't realize the real danger."

"And I think Robin did not consider your knife as a weapon when she borrowed it." Dalton tilted his head and smiled. "I think your very smart and talented daughter needed it for her carving tool, knowing it was sharp and could cause injury if not used carefully. She told me she had gone very slow, knowing the knife was sharp and it took her a long time just to carve the bird. Then she painted it blue with pink highlights to bring out the details." Dalton patted his friend's back "So, have you seen Robin's little blue bird? How did she do?"

"The little blue bird that she placed your carving by? My little six-year-old girl made that?" Joseph smiled, amazed "My friend, I would say Robin takes after her father." He noticed Dalton's sudden confusion and added "Robin's real father!"

CHAPTER 30

"Now, you remember your daddy's reaction when you told him about your little visit with Reverend Lane." Clara could see the tears forming in the young girl's eyes. "Those two fellows were always close to each other and I don't believe there was nothing they wouldn't do to help out the other one, if he truly needed help."

"Yes, I could see that Clara and I can't help but wonder if there is more to it." Robin was dizzy trying to put all the pieces together and she knew if anyone knew the truth, it was Clara. "I don't understand how I could be the only child in this family belonging to Reverend Lane. I thought," she blushed "I thought that maybe mama and Reverend Lane might have had…well, got me before mama married daddy, and he either didn't know she was with child or knew, and raise me as his own."

"Child, just what makes you believe you are Reverend Lanes' only child? Your close resemblance? And who does your brothers and sisters look like? Joseph, your daddy?" Clara sat back smiling.

"You know very well all four, take after mama! Blonde hair and blue eyes! Not a single Stevens child in this house has brown hair." Then it dawned on Robin what Clara was trying to put across to her. "Clara, are you saying, all of us belong to Reverend Lane?"

"Is that what you think I said or is that what you believe?" Clara walked over to see the children laying in their homemade igloo. She chuckled watching Hannah crawl inside. "Sweet child, you should be out there playing in that really cool, and I mean cool, igloo your family just built." Clara moved to one side so Robin could see the other children's handwork. "Pretty good for four little amateurs, would you agree?"

"It is a wonderful igloo, Clara and I just bet Tyler was the head builder."

"Tyler? And why would you assume that, Miss Robin?"

Clara smiled down at the shy girl "Are you looking for a part of your daddy's talent in your brother?"

"Well, daddy was a fine carpenter, Clara." Robin smiled out at the perfectly built ice dwelling. "He could build almost anything he set his mind to."

"Yes, he could, sweet girl and he taught Tyler everything he knew, just like your ancestor Joseph from the good book taught his son Jesus how to be a good carpenter." Clara wrinkled her nose in a smile. "A man does not have to be a son or daughter's flesh and blood daddy to love them or teach them skills to make a good living by. It takes a special person to be a good daddy, and Joseph was one of the best ever."

"Thank you, Clara! I may young but I'm smart enough to understand what message you just gave me, comparing my daddy to Joseph, the earthy father to Jesus." Robin gave Clara a warm hug, her eyes big with questions. "How Clara? How could mama be married to daddy and Reverend Lane be our father?"

"That, my sweet child, is an answer you must wait on until the Lord sees fit for you to know." Clara's eyes held a serious expression that seemed to relax Robin as she added. "Christmas Eve is the night for miracles and who knows what might happen this special Holy night."

Robin had been daydreaming a while longer after her mother had called her downstairs, where Dalton stood waiting to take her to the big birthday party.

"I'm sorry, Dalton! That girl has been in a dream world for weeks now and sometimes she just doesn't hear me call her." Allison reached up and touched his handsome smiling face. "I suppose I should remember how my sister and I used to daydream when we were her age. I think we could be more understanding if we remembered we acted the exact same way."

"I bet you were a cute twelve-year-old, Allison Andersen." Dalton didn't think he could love her more, but it seems to grow stronger with each passing day.

"I wouldn't wager any money on that bet, Reverend Lane." She teased. "My sister and I got into some pretty tight spots."

She laughed softly "Well, mostly Ashley. She was the outgoing one of the two. She loved to sneak out with friends, girls or some of the boys, while I loved reading and helping watch the smaller children when their housemothers needed a helping hand."

"Sounds like, my girl was the little angel and Ashley had a little devilish streak in her." Dalton looked around to make sure they were alone, then gave her a tender kiss. "I cannot see my girl doing anything to gain merits for getting into trouble." He chuckled "Me, I got tons!"

"You? I guess you decided to clean up your act and become a minister then." Allison wanted to hug her true love but was sure Robin had checked her watch and didn't want to be late for her friend's birthday party.

"I didn't exactly decide on my own Allison, the Lord called me one night in the orphanage chapel.

I can't explain it, but I was sitting there while the minister was talking, daydreaming about how I could get my hands on some money to buy a car. I hate to admit it, but I even considered robbing the bank in town."

"Dalton why did you want a car so desperately that you would risk robbing a bank? You could have gone to jail for a very long time or even gotten kill!" Tears filled her luminous blue eyes. "I might never have met you?"

"Well, I never went through with it because the Lord stopped me that night! I felt a hand touch my shoulder and looked up to see no one. Then the cross at the front of the chapel seemed to glow and I heard a voice next to me say, preach the gospel, become one of my lights and minister to my lost sheep, like you have become, my son. Be at peace! Your friend that was lost, has been found."

"Dalton, what did he mean by a friend being lost and was found?" Allison felt the love flowing around them, just as her true love must have felt that night he was called to preach.

"Joseph had gotten in big trouble from cheating on his final exams and the principle told him he would fail the 12th grade and wouldn't get to graduate with his class. My friend had been set up by some bullies that never liked me or Joseph. They slipped the answers to the questions under his notebook. The teacher found it, because the snitch that helped set him up pointed out the slip of paper. Joseph had no idea it was there and he had studied long and hard for the test and knew all but one question. Joseph panicked, and ran away, only adding to his supposing guilt. He called me, scared out of his wits, somewhere in South Carolina, where he had hitch-hiked all the way there. He was afraid, hungry and without any money. He knew he would be in trouble when he got back to the orphanage, but at least he would have someplace to lay his head, and food for his stomach." Dalton looked down at her "He ask me to come get him. He needed his best friend and I needed a car to go after him."

"But the voice said he was found. Did he find a way home?" Allison glanced up at the empty steps, no Robin. "Did Joseph find a ride back to the home."

"This was the strange part Allison, the absolute proof I knew I wasn't imagining the hand on my shoulder, the cross glowing or the calm soft voice speaking in my ear. Joseph walked in the chapel, just as shocked as I was, and we never knew how he got in front of the chapel." Dalton had a faraway look in his eyes for a brief moment, then touched Allison's face.

"I love you, Allison. I have never told anyone that before, afraid they would think me mad, but the minister believed me and so did pop. We told them about Joseph getting set up and after investigating the cheat sheet, the school found who the real cheaters were and Joseph graduated with our class."

"Dalton Lane, I don't see how I could possibly love you anymore!" Allison started to hug him when Robin appeared at the top of the stairs, looking like a Christmas princess. "Oh Dalton, she is beautiful!" she secretly took his hand "Just like her handsome father."

"She is a perfect little doll!" Clara smiled and held out three coats. "Your coat, Dalton, and this pretty green one is for the princess and the red wool one, I believe belongs to you, Allison."

CHAPTER 31

"That Clara, is a real jewel!" Dalton pulled out the chair for Allison and looked around when Ashley and David walked in the café. "David, we're over here."

Smiling, David and Ashley walked over to join the other couple.

"Sometimes I think Bella and Clara are in cahoots with one another." Ashley hugged her sister before sitting down. "Bella kept insisting we come here to try their angel pasta and cream sauce."

"Clara had my red coat ready to leave with Dalton when he took Robin to her friend's big party." Allison laughed as she remembered Clara practically pushing her out the door with Dalton while saying:

"You might as well go along for the ride Allison. It might do you a world of good to get out of this house for some fresh air and good company." Then she smiled up at Dalton "May I suggest that little Italian café across from the Mistletoe and Holly Tavern. I heard the angel pasta is heavenly." And with a twinkle in her eyes, she added "You just might run into some old friends there."

"And I was certain that we would." Allison laughed "And here you both are, right on cue."

"Those two do have a way of brightening up a dreary day." David checked out the wine list. "I say we take their sage advice and enjoy one another's company for the next two hours, until you have to return for your lovely daughter."

"That would be next three hours, my friend." Dalton reached for Allison's hand under the table. "Clara informed us, Robin had a ride home and she would have her lunch ready so she could eat, then be ready for practice when I returned, filled up with good pasta and lots of chit chat!"

"Well, we seem to be among the early dinners, so we shouldn't have to worry about getting ran out for overstaying our welcome." David waved the wine steward over and ordered a bottle of wine then smiled over at Dalton. "My friend, you appear to be as happy as I am."

"I never could be happier, except..." he reached over and kissed Allison's cheek "The day I make this woman my bride."

"I know what you mean. I've wanted to make Ashley my bride for a very long time and finally she wants it too." David put his arm around the beautiful woman.

"We were discussing our youth years, while our daughter was getting ready, and I learned some very interesting things about these identical twins totally different personalities."

"Oh, is that right!" David laughed and sat back. "Let me guess, my Ashley was the most mischievous."

"Very funny, David." Ashley couldn't help but laugh while the wine was poured and she was remembering all the times she had gotten into trouble and her sister bailed her out. "But you're right, I was always getting merits for misbehaving and it almost cost me the roll that made me a star."

"You have my attention, my darling." David took a sip of the good wine and touched her lips "We've got all morning, tell us all about your adventures growing up."

"Being identical twins was, we quickly learned, an advantage over the other orphans. We could switch places if one got into trouble and needed a fill in." Ashley smiled over at her twin, who still looked identical, except for Allison's pale complexion and frail body due to her illness. "I must admit, I was the one who always needed my sister to stand in for me. The bad merits kept coming and stupid me never learned.

The switching started out when we were only ten and I got caught fighting with a town bully who repeatedly threatened the kids in the orphanage. I hit the boiling point when the little creep started hitting my sister.

I had been getting prepared for the day when I could beat the living daylights out of Freddy Bennett. Freddy was the only child of a big shot lawyer in town who stayed so busy with his crooked clients he never had time for his spoiled brat. Freddy's mother was a rich socialite that enjoyed playing with her bridge club over watching after dear mean Freddy. When Doretha wasn't playing bridge, she was playing tennis, golf, or swimming at the Antler Knob Country Club and the kids at the home started calling the rich only club, the Antler Snob Country Club, which I frankly started.

So, while Freddy's parents were busy with their own life, the robust bully, along with his rich friends, would hide and wait for one of the home children walking back from the town library or five and dime. What little money we earned was precious to us and if we could be strong enough to save most of it, we could get a new pair of socks or gloves in the winter time. Besides calling us all names, he would demand us to hand over our meager little coins or maybe a purchase we just made. Getting right up in our face, the spoiled brat would threaten us by declaring he would single handedly beat us to a pulp." Just remembering the mean bully caused Ashley to uncontrollably ball up her fist.

"I was a whole lot smaller than Freddy, so I started working out in our small gym. Mr. Jones, the maintenance man at the orphanage, saw me working out and said he would help me when I told him the reason. He was an amateur boxer and he showed me his moves on an old punching bag he worked out on, behind the gym. When Mr. Jones said I was ready to take on the bully, I just waited for the right time to fight him."

"My very beautiful feminine Ashley Andersen, a boxer?" David slowly ate his salad, enthralled by her captivating story. "A delicate young lady taking on a heavy weight jerk, now, that must have been something to see. Hard to believe."

"It was hard for me to believe as well, David, and I was there and saw everything." Allison recalled what happened the day she had stayed a little longer at the library, trying to find a certain book. "Although now, I cannot remember what it was. Anyway, I was the last to leave, never considering Freddy and his gang would still be out on their bad mission. I was looking down, trying to read and walk back to the children's home when I heard his mocking laugh.

"Well now, if it isn't Miss Bookworm from the dumb children's home!" Freddy laughed out which brought out stickering from his bully friends. "Well, Miss Worm, since I hate to read, you may keep your stupid books, but I will take everything in that little purse over your slimy shoulder."

"I only have 25cents and my library card in here Freddy." Allison stared him in the eye. "Freddy, why do you and your friends always pick on the children from the orphanage all the time? We have never done anything to any of you fellows. It's bad enough picking with the older children, but picking on all those sweet innocent young children is just plain mean and cruel! They run home shaking and crying!"

"Little Miss Bookworm thinks she is a preacher, telling us to stop being mean to all those poor kids from the orphanage." Freddy cocked his head and with a smirk said. "What do you think fellows? Should we just let those poor stupid orphans go down our streets and sidewalks for free?"

"No way Freddy daddy!" the tall skinny boy standing behind their leader spit out. "I say we punish them even more by making them give up their moth-eaten coats!"

"Please fellows, don't you have any feelings? Any compassion for kids who don't have the things you take for granted and enjoy?" Allison's big heart hoped there was a spark of good in Freddy and his gang but all she saw was, six set of eyes filled with hate and mockery.

"The only feelings I'm gonna have is when I knock you on your poor worthless butt!" Freddy took a step toward Allison and was startled when Ashley jumped in front of her sister and put up her fist.

"Hey? What gives? There is two of you?" for a minute, Freddy Bennett was speechless until the big mouth skinny boy spoke up.

"Relax Freddy daddy! You are not seeing double, big cheese! This is those twins I told you about." He bent in close and whispered. "You remember, I said I saw two twins that look exactly the same and they're real lookers? Well, this is them!"

Freddy chuckled, knowing his friend was more into girls than he was. At twelve, Freddy Bennett was just starting to notice girls, but it made no difference to him if he had to beat up a girl instead of a boy, he just enjoyed hurting people.

"Little Orphan Annie, are you trying to scare me with those tight little girly fists?" Freddy turned to his group as they laughed.

"My fist may look little to you, big jerk, but they will give you what for!" Ashley narrowed her eyes as her sister tugged at her arm, begging her to run. "You can leave if you want to Allison, but I'm staying put and beat the crap out of this big bully!"

"Do you hear that, boys? Orphan Annie thinks she can whip my butt!" the robust boy howled in laughter. "A silly, skinny girl, beating me up! That's the funniest thing I have ever heard!"

"My money is on the young lady, fellows!" Mr. Jones stepped up. "How much do you have to wager? If Freddy wins, I will double the bet!"

"Hey mister, you seem mighty sure about Orphan Annie winning! She's just a stupid girl and a poor one at that!" once again, the big mouth skinny boy spoke up.

"That's what makes her chances of winning even higher, young man. She may be a girl, but she is an orphan child, and that makes her touch and more determined to win. Ever since you boys started terrorizing all those orphans, this young lady has been taking notes in her head so she decided it was high time someone stood up to the gang leader." Mr. Jones winked at Ashley as she tried to keep a stern look on her face. "How about that bet boys or are afraid this young lady will win?"

"No way!" Freddy squinted his eyes at the man, not sure how the gang felt about taking a chance with all the money they had taken from the orphans. "But, we cannot bet with you. We don't have any money."

"That's a lot of bull, Freddy Bennett!" Ashley practically yelled. "We have kept track of all the money and items you have stolen from the home kids! On our own, we don't have very much money, but taking every cent from every orphan at Angel of Mercy, it added up to 152 dollars and twenty-two cents, not counting all the items you probably sold!"

"And I see the boy in the back is holding a draw bag, filled with a large amount of coins." Allison had stayed. She would have never left her sister at the mercy of these bullies. "What's the matter fellows? If you are so sure Freddy daddy, the big cheese, will win, you will double your stolen money!" Allison laughed, as Mr. Jones and Ashley joined in. "You know what I think? I believe you aren't really as sure over Freddy daddy winning as you all pretend."

"We'll take that bet, mister! It will be easy money!" Freddy rolled up his sleeves and tightened up his knuckles into two, chubby fist as he sneered. "Alright girlie, get ready to get knocked down!"

"Bring it on Bennett! I've just been waiting to blast your hide to the ground!" Ashley ran up to meet the hardy boy and with one sharp blow on his jaw, Freddy Bennett went flying on the ground. He opened his wild eyes and rubbed his sore jaw, brushing away his gang members as they offered him help in getting up.

"I can manage, darn it!" Freddy flexed his muscles and with a snarl said "Think you're real tough, don't yah, little orphan Annie? I'll show you, dumb girl!"

"Come on and show me, if you think you can hit me, you, big bully!" Ashley got into the position Mr. Jones had taught her and when the heavy boy came charging toward her, she stepped quickly out of his reach and extended her right foot in front of him, sending Freddy Bennett to the ground a second time. "Hey Bennett, laying down on your job?" Ashley howled as a large applause was heard behind her. Some of the orphans had learned about the fight and came to cheer on their hero.

"What's wrong, Freddy, are you going to let a little girl beat you up?" the skinny boy shook his head, feeling disappointed in his gang leader. "Flight like you've been bragging! You're going to make us lose all our cash!"

"Oh no I won't, Conns! Just shut up and stand back while I let this no count orphan have it, right in the gut!" Lowering his head, Freddy charged Ashley like a raving mad bull but before he could smack his big head in her stomach, she lifted up her foot and kicked him backward, knocking him out. His friends turned tail and ran away, leaving their leader in a fallen heap.

CHAPTER 32

"Ashley darling, did you ever get your money back from those cowards that ran away?" David was intrigued over his fiancée's heroic actions.

"After a long debate with Douglas Bennett, Freddy's father, the crooked lawyer." Ashley punched her sister's arm lightly and laughed. "I will never forget the way Norman Randall challenged him in court and won!"

"Who was Norman Randall, another lawyer in town?" Dalton had gotten caught up with their past lives as well. "Was there a jury?"

"Dalton, Norman Randall was a senior at the children's home and had always won the debates at Antler Knob High. He was so smart, a straight A student, and won a full scholarship to Wake Forest University and then another four years at Wake's Law School. Douglas Bennett never stood a chance." Allison squeezed his hand. "And yes, we had a full jury."

"It was obvious that the big bully would go crying to his daddy and blow everything away from the truth." Ashley remembered being nervous when the police officer came calling.

"Ashley, there's a police officer here and he said you had been reported to the department for beating up an innocent young man." Mr. Walker, the headmaster for the orphanage appeared very serious, so I tried to keep my temper down over that ridiculous comment. "Ashley, we will hear what the officer has to say, then you can tell your side of the story. Fair enough?"

"Yes sir, that's fair." Ashley followed the middle-aged man down the hall to his office where the officer was waiting, paper in hand.

"Alright Officer Griffin, tell us what Mr. Bennett had to say about his son, Freddy." Mr. Walter pulled a chair out for Ashley and went behind his desk to open his drawer, then pulled out a file. He sat down and looked up at Griffin.

"Mr. Douglas Bennett came in head courters late yesterday afternoon and file a complaint against Miss Ashley Andersen." Mr. Griffin looked down at the angelic face listening closely to his words. "He states, Miss Andersen picked a fight with his frail son and beat him black and blue."

"That's a bald face lie, sir!" Ashley had held her tongue for as long as she could, after hearing a part of Mr. Bennett's fake report. "Freddy Bennett is about as frail as a work horse! Big as one too!"

The headmaster tried to hide his smile, as the policeman walked over to touch Ashley on the shoulder.

"I'm sure Mr. Bennett was exaggerating over his son's description, Miss Andersen. I have seen 'little' Freddy many times in town with his friends."

"Probably his ex-friends by now sir! They ran away when he lost our fight and took their stolen money with them!" Ashley suddenly felt brave, because she knew, even though fighting was wrong, she did it for a good cause.

"Stolen money? Mr. Bennett claims you tried to make his son give you their clubs money." The officer tried not to smile at the looks the young ten-year-old was giving him.

"They might have called it their club's money, Officer Griffin, but the six thieves took it from all the orphans they stopped and scared into handing over their few pennies." She twisted her lip and added "And just to set the record straight, I did not beat Freddy Bennett black and blue! I just gave him a sore jaw, sore knees, and one fat bruised butt!"

Jimmy Griffin had to turn his head to hide his soft chuckle and he was sorry he had missed out on seeing the fight between this tough little girl and that chubby spoiled brat.

"Excuse me sir." Norman Randall had been walking by Mr. Walter's office when he saw the police officer waiting. He had found a safe place to listen and chuckled to himself several times from young Ashley's comments. "You have the right to remain quiet Ashley and I, as your lawyer, will see to it that we put an end to that little bully and his heathen gang, once and for all."

"Are you prepared to take on Mr. Douglas Bennett, young man?" Officer Griffin admired all the young people at the orphanage and he had heard about Norman's ability to win debates at high school. "This is not just another class assignment, Mr. Randall. You will be dealing with a real experienced lawyer and a legal court. Are you prepared to go before a judge and lay out your case against professionals?"

"I will lay out my case, Sir, in front of a twelve- person jury!" Norman winked at Ashley, who was smiling from ear to ear. "We have all the evidence we need to win this case and before I'm finished with that lying, cheating family, the entire town will be thanking us!"

"We did have a trial and when I walked in the courtroom with Norman, Freddy Bennett gave me a wicked smile, while his crooked lawyer father, faked a smile at Norman and said, "Good luck son, you're going to need it." Ashley put her head over on David as she told what happened.

"The courtroom was filled with a lot of the town's people and a few children from the orphanage, so they could testify about getting bullied and robbed by Freddy and his gang. The very smallest children would be kept at the home, due to the trauma caused by the rough gang. The twelve jury members consisted of six men and six women, all from a neighboring town, just to keep it fair. The Bennett's were not all that liked in Antler Knob and most of the town people were plainly on the side of the children's home. So, Douglas Bennett was called on to give his opening statements."

"Ladies and gentlemen of the jury, it grieves me that we are here today to prove that a small child…" Bennett turned with flare and pointed at Ashley, then continued "That small girl deliberately beat up Freddy Bennett. If you look at this innocent looking young lady, you might observe there are no bruises on her delicate fair skin. Now I ask you to look at my client, and you will notice bruises on his face, his knees, and if I were to ask him to remove his clothes, you would also see bruises on his buttocks. The reason for the girl being without bruises and Freddy Bennett being covered in bruises, is because my client did not touch that young girl. She attacked him for no apparent reason except to rob him and his club members of their meager dues."

Norman touched Ashley and placed his finger over her mouth, knowing she was about to object herself, so he whispered he would not interrupt Bennett's opening statements and he would expect the same respect and ask the judge to let him have the floor, uninterrupted. Ashley settled down as she watched the crooked lawyer at work.

"One might ask how such a small girl could beat up a boy, two- years her senior and serval pounds heavier." Hearing Ashley laugh at his statement, he turned to stare at her. Ashley gave him a sweet smile, causing him to look away and continue. "Her strength comes from being possessed by something evil and wicked."

"My sister is not evil or wicked! Your son and his gang are!" Allison spoke up and the judge called her forward.

"Young lady, I know you do not know the rules inside my courtroom, but you really need to restrain yourself from speaking out." The judge looked down on the exact copy of the girl on trial. "I can see that Ashley is your twin sister and I know you feel the need to defend and protect her, but I'm asking you nicely, please, no more outburst like that again or I will have to ask your housemother to escort you out of my courtroom. Do you understand?"

"Yes sir. I'm sorry if I broke your rules but I love my sister with all my heart and she is a really good person, your honor."

The judge reached down and patted her blonde hair and said softly "I know you love you sister, child. I love my sister too and I understand how hard it would be for me to sit still and not take up for her, but you will try really hard, won't you. We need you to testify later on. Okay?"

Allison smiled and went back to her seat as Mr. Bennett leaned into the jury. "Ladies and gentlemen, please strike from your thoughts the comments of Miss Allison Andersen. The girl will say anything to save her sister from going to juvenile detention. Young people who are not right in the head tend to be dangerous to society and need help and that is why I ask you to listen to the witnesses I will call, then decide for yourselves weather or not this girl is guilty of beating up an innocent boy."

"Mr. Randall, you may give your opening statement now." The judge sat back to listen, as his attention kept going back to the children in question. Freddy Bennett made a face at the ten-year-old and she, in return, stuck out her tongue at him. The judge put a hand over his mouth to hide his smile, as the young man walked up to the twelve men and women.

"Ladies! Gentlemen! I am here today to prove that the real troublemaker seated before you is Freddy Bennett and not my client. Let me start by saying, ten-year-old Ashley Andersen, did in fact have a fight with Freddy Bennett, but her reasons are legit. Once you hear all the evidence and hear my witnesses, you can judge who is to blame for this little girl's decision. I'm sure you have noticed Master Bennett and his five friends are all dressed today in their suits. And by the looks of them, I would say they are brand new." The group of twelve looked over at the boys and noticed a tag tangling from one of their coats and tried not to laugh when the boy beside him yanked it off. "I will prove these six boys have been bulling serval children from the Angel of Mercy Orphanage, from ages ten to three-years-old for a very long time and threating to beat them up if they don't hand over their money. To some of you fine folks, 25 cents is not very much, but the younger children only get a few pennies a day for doing little things and they save their pennies until they get twenty-five cents, then they can buy a coloring book or a box of crayons at the five and dime or maybe some chewing gum or a comb. Those who are thrifty and save their quarters, can buy a new pair of gloves or socks without holes. So, this meager little amount is a lot to an orphan who doesn't have anything. When the very youngest children are targeted by these bullies, they have nightmares of being robbed then beat up by the gang. Yes, Ashley Andersen decided to fight the leader of this gang and put an end to the bulling and stealing."

"Ladies and Gentlemen, you have heard the opening statements by both parties and now we will hear from the witnesses." The Judge's eyes fell on Freddy Bennett, then to his father. "Mr. Bennett, you may call your first witness."

Giving Hearts

"I call Steve Conns to the witness stand." Douglas Bennett patted the skinny boy on the back as he walked behind the wall and stared down at the Bible placed in front of his hands, then looked up at the clerk.

"Please place your hand on the Bible." The stiff clerk waited until Steve placed a nervous hand on the Holy Book. "State your full name." the skinny boy gave his name "Do you solemnly swear to tell the truth, the whole truth, and nothing but the truth, so help you God?"

"A...yes?" Mr. Bennett whispered I will, and the nervous boy said, "I will."

"You can relax Steve, no one here expects a young boy to know how a court runs." Bennett gave him a reassuring smile. "Now, tell me, have you or your fellow club members every stopped any of those poor little orphans and threatened them if they didn't give you their money?"

"Oh, no sir. We never even go near that place. Besides, we get plenty of money from our parents from the allowances they give us. You know, you give Freddy a hundred dollars a month, sir. Why would we want to take those helpless little orphan's pennies?" Steve Conn tried to look sincere.

"You boys stay pretty busy during the summer vacation, don't you? Please tell the court what keeps you fellows too busy to think about getting into mischief." Bennett rubbed his chin, hoping this kid had some imagination.

"Gosh, Mr. Bennett, sir, we stay plenty busy all day. In the mornings we get together at Freddy's house, you know, your house sir. That's where we have our club meeting before going to the country club to swim. Then we have a cheeseburger there before we hit the tennis court. Later on, we go to the gym and shoot a few hoops." Conns raised his shoulders. "You know, just hang and stay out of trouble sir."

"Thank you, Steve. I have no more questions." Mr. Bennett walked back to his seat as Steve Conns started to jump up.

"Just hold on there, young man. Please sit back down until I see if Mr. Randall wants to cross examine you." The judge pushed up his glasses then turned to Norman. "Mr. Randall, would you care to question this witness?'

"Yes sir, I do." Norman smiled down at the nervous boy, who was pulling at his shirt collar. "Did you buy the wrong size shirt, Steve? It appears that collar is about to choke off your wind."

"I think I grabbed the wrong size this morning." The kid looked up startled, knowing he had made a slip up.

"I see! Yes, I suppose when you have to pick out clothes in a hurry to make sure you look respectful in the courtroom, that can be hard for a group of fellows who live in jeans and t-shirts all summer." Norman stopped when Bennett objected, but the judge overruled it.

"Mr. Bennett, I see nothing wrong with Mr. Randall's statement. It is clear to everyone present that these suits were just purchased and I have no doubt that these boys had rather wear jeans and t-shirts, right young man?"

"Yes sir, I'd much rather wear my jeans and club t-shirt over this suit sir." Steve Conn couldn't understand why Freddy and his daddy where frowning at him, so he looked back up at the young man questioning him. "Mr. Bennett just wanted us to look nice in the courthouse, like we do at church."

"Do you attend church regularly son?" Norman asked.

"I go whenever the folks go, sir. About once a month."

"Steve, do you understand when you placed your hand on the Bible, you weren't just telling this courtroom you would tell the truth, but you were telling God." Norman laid his hands on the rail in front of the nervous boy. "Now son, you said you never went near the orphanage, didn't you?"

"That's right! We never go near the place." He looked up cocky.

"Then you never saw Ashley Andersen hit Freddy Bennett, did you?" Norman smiled at his big eyes. "What's wrong Steve? Did you or did you not see my client hit your friend?"

"A…yes sir, but…I can explain! The guys decided to walk a different way home on Tuesday evening and it happened to pass that home for unwanted children." Steve swallowed, hoping this man would not ask him another question because he kept digging himself deeper in a hole.

"To set the record straight, young fellow, the orphans at the home are not unwanted. I would go as far to say, no doubt there are some unrulily children that parents would prefer to not have." Norman smiled when he heard the seasoned lawyer grunt. "Let me guess, you fellows were just strolling along minding your own business when this petite young lady crossed your path and provoked an argument?"

"A…yeah, something like that. We had met her sister first and was having a friendly conversation. Her sister was really helpful, giving us some good advice and all. Then Miss Ashley Andersen came charging up, all mad and ready to get into a fight!"

"I'm curious Steve. Why would a young girl you have never met wish to start a fight with you boys?" Norman knew the young man had become frozen as he stumbled for words.

"I…I…I'm not rightly sure."

"No more questions." The soon to be lawyer smiled down when the boy let out his breath when the judge told him to step down.

"I call Freddy Bennett to the stand." Douglas Bennett walked his son up to the chair and watched as he marched behind the stand and motioned for the clerk holding the Bible. "I'm, ready!"

CHAPTER 33

"Freddy, will you tell this court what happened on Tuesday, June the 18th."

"Yes, you bet I will!" He pulled some bubblegum out of his pocket and gram it in his mouth, despite his father's shaking head. "Cool it pop! I just need to wet my whistle!"

"Young man, I must ask you to respect my court." The judge peered over his glasses. "Mr. Pearman, collect the young man's gum and dispose it in the waste can." The clerk carried a trash can over and held out a tissue for the bubble gum. Freddy chomped it for one more second before taking it out and sticking it on the man's hand.

"Woops! I missed!" the robust twelve-year-old faked a smile at the angry little clerk, who walked away pulling the sticky mess from his hand. "Alright, pop, let's get this over with! I've got plans this afternoon and I don't want to miss them by sitting in this stuffy old building having my gum taken away!"

Douglas Bennett forced a smile at the serious judge, then frowned down at his spoiled son.

"Young man, one more smart remark, I will ground you the rest of the summer! Now, do you need for me to repeat my question?"

"What was I doing on Tuesday, June 18th!" The rude boy rolled his eyes. "Me and the club gang had done everything Slim Bean Conns stated earlier. You know, our club meeting, then swimming, having a big lunch at the country club, tennis, then hoops at the gym! It was my ideal to walk by that children's home, cause, me and the boys felt real sad for all those poor children and had heard about a rough gang harassing them helpless little children, even taking their pitiful amount of coins." Freddy let out a sorrowful sigh. "We decided we would become the silent knights, check out the lay of the land, then hide and wait for the sorry bandits and put an end to their reign of terror, secretly! You know, unknown heroes, like Zorro or the Long Ranger!"

"Can you tell the jury what cause the young lady to punch you in the face, then trip you, knocking you down, bruising your knees before she kicked you to the ground again, causing unconsciousness." Douglas walked over to the jury, then turned to face his son. "Now, Freddy, take your time and tell us everything that happened before and during the confrontation with Ashley Andersen."

"Like I said, me and the fellows had talked it over and decided the best way to stop the bulling was to help those poor helpless orphans. Our good source told us where and when the mean gang would strike so we had to go check things out. This blue eye blonde was out walking by herself so we felt the need to follow her, just in case that gang was hiding in wait ahead. She befriended us, just like Conns told you, and started preaching…giving us some advice about the mean gang, when out of the blue, her sister rush up holding out her fist, right in my face. I talked real sweet to the angry young girl, but she said: My fist might be small but they will give you what for! I was still trying to explain things to her when out of the blue, she socked me in the face, knocking me silly." The heavy boy narrowed his eyes at Ashley before continuing "I ain't never hit a girl before and I wasn't figuring on doing it then, so I decided our best solution was to turn tail and run. When I started past her, the little devil stuck her foot out and tripped me, causing me to fall on my knees, hard!" Freddy looked over at the jury helplessly. "What else could I do?

"I couldn't just stay there and let her keep hurting me and all we wanted to do was help the orphans." Freddy peered down, as though he were ashamed of what he had done. "It was her or me, but I didn't want to hurt the sick girl, just bump her out of the way so we could leave. Putting my head down, I ran toward her and that's when the crazy girl gave me a karate kick, knocking me back on my rear, where I blacked out."

"And that's why you have been carrying that soft pillow around with you today, right son?" The lawyer seemed pleased with the boy's statement.

"That's right, sir. The doctor said my butt was badly bruised and suggested I sit on a pillow when I wasn't standing." Freddy made a painful face, mostly for the jury. "The problem is, my knees are so sore, it hurts to stand, even walk!"

"Which is why we will be asking for a small settlement, since it is the orphanage's responsibility and their funds are limited. At least the boy's doctor bills and torn clothing should be covered. I would never dream of asking a home for orphan children to give us the large settlement we could retain for physical and mental abuse." Douglas smiled at his son as he said, "No more questions." He cockily faked a smile at the opposing amateur attorney feeling confident in his son.

"Your turn for questions, Mr. Randall."

"Thank You, Mr. Bennett." Norman stepped up in front of the obnoxious juvenile as stared down until the rude young man stopped pretending to ignore him by looking around the courtroom and rolled his eyes over at him. "Now, that I have your attention, Master Bennett, First, let me congratulate you for such a spell binding report. It would appear, by the descriptions you and your friend, Steve Conns gave, all you boys are decent and caring young men. Would you agree with that statement?"

"Sure thing! We are probably the friendliest and most helpful young men in the entire town!" Freddy looked out at his friends. "Right boys?" a loud "yes," came from the 5 boys listening as the judge banged his wooden hammer down and stared out at the five young men.

"We will have order in this courtroom! If there is another outburst like that again, I will have you ushered out to the hallway!" He turned to the boy sitting in the witness chair. "I will warn you one last time, Master Bennett, if you say or do anything that rubs me the wrong way, you will be the one on trial here. Do I make myself clear?"

Freddy dropped his head, anger written on his face as he mumbled "Yes sir!"

"Now, you stated earlier that you had a hard time sitting, standing and walking. Is that correct?" Norman was glad to have Garland Shelton as the judge, knowing he was just and honest and not one to cater to William Douglas Bennett's bribery.

"That's correct! Sitting is a pain in the butt and standing is even worse!" Freddy looked pitiful over at the jury "Why, I can hardly put one foot in front of the other!"

"Are you sure you want to stick to that answer, Freddy?" Norman walked over by the six men and six women, glancing back at the cocky young man on the stand. "Is it really difficult for you to walk or are you just lying to this jury?"

"I object your honor!" Douglas Bennett flew to his feet. "My client has stated he is in pain and it is difficult for him to walk! I ask that Mr. Randall's last remark be stricken from the records!"

Judge Shelton called both attorneys up to the bench. "Mr. Randall, is there a reason for calling this boy a liar?"

"It is your honor. From something that happened just a few minutes ago, sir. I can prove he is giving false testimony in the case." Norman felt good about the outcome while Mr. Bennett was getting railed up. The judge observed both men, then said, "Overruled! Proceed with you questioning Mr. Randall."

"Freddy, when you were called up to the witness stand, everyone in this courtroom, including your lawyer, saw you march up to the witness stand. It was obvious that you were in no pain." Norman bent down close to the boy "Would you like to rephrase your answer? Does your legs hurt to stand or walk?"

"Okay! So, the pain went away! It did hurt! I swear it!" Freddy suddenly felt anxious when the young acting lawyer picked up the Bible. "As I recall Freddy, you also swore on this Holy Book, to tell the truth, the whole truth and nothing but the truth. Is there something else wrong with your statements? Isn't it a fact that you fellows were waiting for one of the orphans to come along and scare into giving you their money? Something you had been doing all summer until Ashley Andersen had enough and decided to stand up to the lead bully, you. She jumped in when you and your gang were harassing her sister, who was trying to convince you six boys to change your ways but the hate you had for the poor orphans blinded her sweet words. You had been asking for a fight, knowing that the kids you targeted were younger and smaller than you."

"No! That is not true! I am a good boy and I don't lie!" Freddy shouted "Ashley Andersen is just a little snot nose orphan! Why, I should have knock her…"

"Knocked her down, like you did some of the smaller children because they started crying and wouldn't shut up when you gave the order!" Norman kept his cool as he moved back to the jury, then looked up at the judge. "No more questions for this witness, for now."

"You may return to your seat and if you have any more witnesses, Mr. Bennett, you may call them now." Judge Shelton shuffled papers on his desk as the depressed lawyer mumbled, "I have no more witnesses, your honor." Douglas Bennett frowned down at his son, holding back the urge to slap him.

After the judge told Norman, your witnesses, he called Mr. Jones to the stand.

"I am the janitor for the Angel of Mercy Orphanage and have been for the past twenty years. There is no better bunch of kids than the ones growing up there. Their manners are sweet and precious. That's why, one day a couple weeks ago, I saw Ashley Andersen trying to do the barbells, used mostly by the high school boys. They would do as many chin lifts as they could manage, and being strong boys, they got their count on up there. Now this little girl had found her a box to climb up on, so she reached the rail and I watched her trying real hard to lift herself up. After making three successful chin lifts, I figured I best stop her before she ups and hurts herself. She commenced to telling me she needed to build her muscles and learn how to fight so she could whoop Freddy Bennett and his gang. Now, I had been hearing about that group of bullies harassing some of the kids at the home and stealing what little money they had and even things they had bought themselves, so I took it upon myself to show that little girl how to defend herself in a fight."

"Mr. Jones, is it true you are an amateur boxer and have even won a few trophies?" Norman always liked the quiet custodian and use to have long chats with him watching him hit the punching bag in behind the gym.

"I am and that's why I knew I could train this little girl the basic steps in boxing and even some karate. We placed that box she used up at my punching bag and after I strapped up her hands, that gal learned real fast!" Mr. Jones winked at his little boxing student. "I knew she was ready to take on Freddy Bennett. I had seen him in the local pharmacy put away a four-scoop bowl of ice cream, topped with hot fudge and whipped cream then order the waitress at the counter to cover it with a dozen cherries." He laughed softly "He was a different kind of heavy weight, if you catch my meaning and I knew one good blow, would topple him to the ground."

"Did you happen to see the fight?" Norman knew he had and now the jury would know a grownup had witness everything that happened.

"I followed Ashley, wanting to be sure the other five boys wouldn't jump her while she was fighting the big bully. I heard the threats Freddy Bennett made and the name calling. He had called Miss Allison, a slimy book worm, because she had a book from the library and he had nicknamed Ashley, little orphan Annie. He kept calling her bluff and I noticed a red haired, freckled boy watching from the back of the pack. Then I saw he had a leather bag strapped around his neck and every time he moved, the contents would clang together."

"And what would your guess be, Mr. Jones? What could possibly clang together every time the boy moved with excitement?" Norman Randall saw the boy in question slide down in his seat and knew he would be his next witness.

"I'd say it looked and sounded like a bag on coins." He scratched his beard "Yep, it was coins alright. That's when I got the bright idea to make a bet with the gang that the girl would win the fight and, if she lost, I would give them double what they had in their money bag. The leader wasn't as sure about winning as his five gang members and tried to make excuses for not betting, but that shinny boy, I think I heard Bennett call him Steve Conns, he told Freddy to go ahead and show them what he had always bragged about.

Ashley and Freddy made a charge for one another, but

Ashley's swift fist made a perfect punch, right on the bully's right jaw, knocking him to the ground. Oh, he was really mad then and managed to stand up without any help from his friends, who he brushed away. Freddy pushed up his sleeves and made a run for Ashley, who made a quick step back, foot out move, that sent the red face boy on his knees. Trying one more time, with even angrier remarks, Freddy put his head down like a bull, fingers for horns, and made the charge. My brilliant student was waiting with the defensive karate kick that finished off her competitor and his brave gang members ran away with their bag of stolen money."

"Objection! The witness is only speculating about the boy's bag. It is merely his guess that the contents in that bag was coins, much less stolen money. Nonsense! The bag is probably nothing but a bag of marbles, the boys have collected over their years together." Douglas Bennett was getting desperate as he added "I recall my son telling me his club is called the Marble Head Boys or something to that nature." Red faced, he turned to the judge "I ask that Mr. Jones' comments about the bag be removed from the notes."

"It is just your guess, Mr. Jones, that the bag contained coins, so, until we know for certain, we shall strike those remarks from the court records and I would ask that the jury ignore that remark." The judge looked with passion at the young man, defending the young girl. "Do you have any more questions for this witness?"

"Yes, just one please." Norman knew he had one step back about the gang's purse, but he would soon know what was in the bag when he called the red-headed boy up. "Mr. Jones, I am going to ask you, for this court, this jury and all the witnesses here, can you point out the six boys who you just describe?"

"Yes sir, I can." Mr. Jones pointed to the five boys wearing new suits, all with their heads down, then he pointed at their leader, Freddy Bennett. "Those are the six boys I saw harassing the two twin girls, who are also seated in the courtroom."

"Thank you, Mr. Jones. I have no more questions." After Norman sit down, Douglas Bennett declined to counter examine the witness, so Mr. Jones stepped down.

"I call Willy Cline to the stand." Norman waited as the red headed boy nervously stood up and made his way slowly to the witness stand and gave his pledge on the Bible, then felt for the chair before sitting down.

"Willy, there's no reason for you to be nervous. All you have to do is tell the truth when I ask you a few simple questions about your part in the fight that occurred on Tuesday, June the 18th. You might as well admit you were there, Willy. I know you saw the witnesses that arrived after the fight started, didn't you?"

"Witnesses? After the fight?" the boy swallowed hard before adding "I saw that Jones man, the one that made the bet."

"Think Willy, I know you remembered seeing all those little faces standing just inside the children's home entrance. They had heard about the fight and snuck out to see for themselves Ashley, one of their own, taking on Freddy Bennett, the one who had scared them and taken their money." Norman got down to look the boy in the eye. "They saw you watching them, so they stood real still, hoping none of the other boys would notice then watching. You might as well tell the truth. They described you, the smaller boy in the back with red hair and freckles."

Willy looked out and saw his mother had come in the courtroom and knew she was a good mother to him, not like the other club member's mothers, who ignored them. Seeing her face looking sad over the situation, he knew he had to break his brother's code of silence and tell the truth, even if it meant losing his friends.

"I did see children watching, a lot of children. They looked real scared so I didn't say nothing to my club brothers."

"Willy, why didn't you want the other boys to know about the children watching?" Norman felt good that one of these boys had some compassion and was finally telling the truth.

"I don't know. I was scared for those kids, I guess. Sometimes the boys talk tough and I just didn't want an innocent child to get hurt, so I kept quiet." He looked out at the mad faces on his friend's then noticed Freddy's father had laid his head down on the desk.

Joan Byrd

"So, Willy, what was your part of the fight?" Norman knew he had an honest witness so the questions would be stepped up a notch.

"Gee sir, I would never fight anyone! Freddy is the president of our club, sir, and he is the one who does all the talking." Willy looked out at his leader and noticed the double fist and the squint in his eyes. Norman turned to see what had him nervous and Freddy quickly looked down.

"Son, you do not have to be afraid of Freddy Bennett. Of all the members in your club, you are the bravest. It takes a strong person to go against a group of boys and tell the truth so an innocent girl's charges will be dismissed and the guilty party be made to pay, you being the exception." Norman smiled down at the young boy, feeling free, at long last. "The truth is that Freddy is the only one who fights and makes threats, is that correct?"

"Yes sir! Freddy is always pushing the rest of us around and telling us what to do." This time Will looked out at the leader, unafraid and ready to tell everything. "It was all Freddy's ideal to harasses those poor orphans and threaten to beat them up unless they handed over their coins.

"I was the treasurer and I carried the bag to put the coins in." the red headed boy looked down and shook his head. "Golly-gee, Mr. Randall, I wanted to fit in and be part of the club. I never knew Freddy had this mean streak until after I joined the group, then he decided to start scaring the younger orphans and take their money. He even changed the name of the club to the coin gang instead of the marvel shooters!" The boy looked out sadly at Freddy's father. "Mr. Bennett was pretty close to the old club name."

"Thank you, Willy, for telling the truth." Norman Randall patted his red head as he looked back to see the boy's mother smiling. "I wouldn't worry none about finding new friends Willy. Perhaps, you might start at the orphanage. The kids there are super nice and capable of having a good time with their friends. An outsider is always welcome." He was rewarded with a big smile as he concluded "No more questions."

"Mr. Randall, do you have anymore witnesses?" The judge

felt the case had been thoroughly laid out and was ready for the closing arguments. Judge Garland Shelton waited until the young man spoke with his young client, then stood back up.

"If it would please the court, my client, Miss Ashley Andersen, wishes a moment of the court's time, to give her testimony." Norman helped the girl to her feet and waited on the judge to speak.

"This is pretty much an open and shut case, Mr. Randall, and the evidence has been laid out before this jury, but if Miss Ashley fills the need to defend herself or just speak her mind, the court will grant a five minute or less statement from Miss Andersen."

Joan Byrd

CHAPTER 34

"I would like to thank Willy for being honest about Freddy Bennett and the other club members for targeting the kids at the orphanage since the beginning of summer vacation. I am sure if you count the money in their treasury bag it would match the amount reported to our headmaster as stolen. I will admit to striking Freddy Bennett three times, but that is only because I was too fast for the big bully. Believe me, if Freddy could fight as good as he pretended, I would have been knocked out, maybe." Those on the jury tried not to laugh when Ashley added. "I never worried about the overweight loser hitting me because he was so fat he almost wobbled when he tried to walk. It would be kinda like knocking over bowling pin or a drunk duck!" Ashley looked out at Freddy, who had narrowed his eyes at her description of him. Then he sat up and listened as she changed her speech into another direction.

"I am old enough to know Willy's testimony decided the outcome in this case and I feel certain that I will be found not guilty, just as sure as I believe Freddy and the other gang members, 'cept for Willy, will have to go to juvenile detention for the remainder of the summer or even longer for harassing innocent children and stealing their money. I am asking the jury and the court to reconsider their verdict and put the blame on the parents of these boys. They are left unsupervised all summer and probably all year, for that matter. I guess we kids at the home are pretty lucky after all, cause we got angels who love us and take care of us. If we misbehave, they are there to correct us, because they genially care and want us to become good children who will later become good adults." The small girl walked over to Douglas Bennett and looked down.

"Mr. Bennett, sir, when is the last time you told Freddy you loved him? Or ask him how his day went, took some time to shoot hoops with him or take him to a football or baseball game?" As Ashley asked her questions, Freddy looked over at

158

his father, hoping to see a little compassion or a hint of fatherly love. As she waited and received no response, her eyes fell on the robust boy watching his heartless father, hoping for a glimpse of real parental affection. Her young heart went out to the young boy as she reached over and touched his hand. "I understand the hurt you are feeling Freddy. Your family have a lot of money and could buy you anything you want, but it isn't the material things you need, is it? It's knowing your parents truly love you and show it with a hug or a little praise for doing something you've accomplished."

Freddy looked up at his one-time foe as real tears filled his eyes when she said, "Why did you hate the orphans, Freddy? Did you assume we were just like you, without the love of parents and you needed to strike out at someone less fortunate? Did you not know, we had what you had been looking for all your life!"

"The orphans were always laughing and happy, making their way to the five and dime to buy a cheap item. I had expected to see them down and blue, having no parents and very little money, but instead, just a simple 25 cent coloring book brought out such joy and excitement, I wanted to scream. I wanted them to be miserable like me, no parent to love them, rebellious and filled with unrulily behavior. Instead, I found them content with their life and very disciplined in their manners. I would meet them on the street and get a friendly smile, nod, or wave and I kept repeating, they are poor orphans, they have no right to be happy! I will take away their smiles and their pennies, then they will be as miserable as me!" Freddy could feel his father watching him and knew he probably felt like hitting him again, but he just didn't care anymore what his father thought as he burst out "You're right, Ashley Andersen, I wanted what you had! I wanted to be happy, filled with joy and loved by someone! It hurts when you ask for things and your parents supply them just to keep you busy and out of their hair but...they have never given me what I really wanted!"

"What's that Freddy?" Douglas Bennett felt sure the judge would stop this girl's long speech by now, but he had never seen his son cry before and some fatherly emotion clicked inside him. "Tell me what it is you want son, and your mother and I will give it to you."

Freddy had not looked over at his father, afraid he would make fun of his answer, so he looked at Ashley for an answer.

"Just tell him Freddy. Tell your daddy what's in your heart." Ashley teared up as she hugged her old enemy. "If my daddy and mama was still alive, I know I would tell them how much I loved them."

"I never considered your mama and daddy were dead Ashley." As everyone present looked on, Freddy Bennett got up to hug the young girl, then turned to his father. "Daddy, the one thing I want most in the world, is for you and mama to love me, the way I love you." The boy couldn't tell what his father was thinking from the cold stare, so he added "It's alright if you can't say it sir. I'm pretty much used to it by now. I guess it's because you don't love me and I'm just a big disappointment to you or maybe you never really wanted me in the first place. If that's the case sir, I will ask you for one more thing, please place me in the Angel of Mercy orphanage, where real love grows and I can finally find the happiness I've been searching for."

"For the very first time in his twelve years on earth, young Freddy Bennett felt his father take him in his arms weeping and told the boy what he had been needing to hear." Ashley smiled up at David, who seemed caught up in the adventures of his fiancé. "My mischief didn't stop there but Allison was always there to bail me out. Like the time I really wanted to attend our summer camp retreat because Miss Macy Martin was going to be there to lead a class on acting. She had volunteered and taught at the local arts school. No matter how hard I tried to stay out of trouble, I ended up with one or two demerits every week to Allison's zero merits. She was a model student and a perfect young lady."

"Sounds like my girl hasn't changed all that much, still a perfect little angel." Dalton checked his watch and noticed they had a good hour left. "So, Ashley, I take it, you never got to go to camp."

"Oh, I went, thanks to my saintly sister, who took my place, pretending to be me and I went as Allison." Ashley laughed "It was a good thing we knew how to act. Everyone at camp thought I was Allison and sweet Allison had everyone fooled at the home, thinking I was moping around because I missed out on the acting class."

"And in return, my wonderful actress sister, had everyone believing I had promised to sit in the acting class and take notes for poor Ashley instead of attending the painting class which I sighed up for." Allison took a sip of the freshly made coffee as she remembered another time.

CHAPTER 35

"It was our senior year and we knew we would be leaving the safety of the home to find a life on the outside. Ashley had never given up her desire to become an actress, so an opportunity came when she tried out for the lead role in the town theater and won it hands down. The play was Romeo and Juliet and Ashley rehearsed her lines for me so many times, I knew them by heart. So, when Mr. Jarvis, the Antler Knob Theater's director asked me to be her stand in, I said yes, remembering Ashley had only two unused merits left and if she slipped up, she would be grounded and not allowed to perform in the play."

"I had been the perfect little saint, watching my every move so I wouldn't get my last two merits." Ashley could remember turning down several chances to take in a movie down on main, which wasn't against the rules if one got back by eight. The problem was, the movie usually let out at seven, giving plenty of time to walk back to the home, but if you stopped for a quick burger, you might run late and get caught sneaking in. "Allison and I had saved up some money, doing little jobs around the neighborhood, like Cleaning someone's house, or doing their washing and ironing. By putting our money together, we had just enough to pay Roy Brown, from Brown's Home Movies, to come to the theater the night of the dress rehearsal and film me doing Juliet."

"Everything was working out beautifully. Mr. Brown had agreed to film Ashley's scenes and make several copies so she could send them to some film producers in Hollywood. She had hoped one of them might think she was talented enough to come out to Hollywood and save her from having to find a job to make enough money to attend the local school of the arts." Allison glanced over at her sister and shook her head. "Then the movie house downtown changed the movie on Thursday night instead of Saturday and it just happened to be the one

Ashley had been dying to see."

"Uh-Oh! I know where this is going." David laughed "Please, tell me you didn't."

"I'm afraid I did. My friends Marty, Ron, and Buddy decided to go with the good intentions of getting back by eight." Ashley made a face at David and Dalton, when they both laughed. "Real cute fellows, but you're right, I messed up really bad. The movie wasn't as good as I had imagined, so, to cheer me up, the gang took me to Joes burgers for a cheeseburger and a beer, which was a great big no-no, if you got caught drinking. I should have known better since the rest of my group didn't have as many merits as I had and didn't have the lead role in Romeo and Juliet. Checking our watches, we had only fifteen minutes to walk home, which normally took twenty-five. We decided to run and of course, it started raining which made the ground slick. My boots started slipping on the hill above the orphanage and the next second I was sliding down the hill, like a skier, trying hard to keep my balance. Just as I reached the bottom, the main door flew opened and I landed right in Mr. Walker's arms."

"The Mr. Walker? The man in charge of the orphanage?" David burst out laughing. "I can only guess, but I assume you got both merits for being late, drinking and landing in the headmasters' arms."

"That is exactly what happened and to make sure Allison or I didn't change places, we had to wear two different color uniforms all day Friday to make sure we wouldn't change places for the dress rehearsal that night and my big chance to get filmed."

"Sometimes being identical twins is an advantage, even though Mr. Walker and the home board had thought the whole thing through, or so they thought." Allison began to tell the story of what happened. "To make sure they could tell us apart to start with, Mrs. Fleming, our housemother, came into our room, first thing Friday morning with the two different uniforms and to decide which twin wore which color."

"Allison?" Ellen Fleming knew Allison always wore a small gold cross around her neck, a gift from her grandmother

Andersen, before she passed away when the girls were fourteen, so seeing it dangle from her pajamas, she handed her the blue uniform. The loving housemother gazed sadly down Ashley, who always platted her hair at night in a long single pigtail. She held out the black uniform with strict instructions for both girls.

"Young ladies, identical twins have been known to switch places to help one another out and up until now, we haven't seen any strong reasons for you, Allison, to perhaps, switch with Ashley, even though she had to miss out on things. We feel this time is different, knowing how much the play has meant to you, Ashley, but you did break house rules. I know it isn't easy to let Ashley take over for you as Juliet, but she is well-prepared and Mr. Jarvis said he had full confidence in his stand in." Mrs. Fleming rung her hands nervously as she gave out their rules for both Friday and Saturday. "To make sure you will never be alone together at any time, to switch uniforms or personal jewelry, there will be an adult with each of you at all times. Tonight, you will be placed in separate bedrooms with your adult guardian, where she will lock the door and hold the key."

The housemother gave them a weak smile and asked, "Do you have any questions about your arrangement?"

"I think we understand, Mrs. Fleming." Ashley looked over at her sister. "I know I broke the rules ma'am and I'm really sorry. Even though it hurts me deeply not to be at dress rehearsal tonight or the performance tomorrow night, I confess it is really all my fault and I will abide by your strong rules. I just think that it is unfair that my sister be treated like a criminal for something I did."

"Sometimes when we break rules Ashley, others we love are recipients to our bad behavior and in your case, must face the same punishment or to put it kinder, the same arrangement." The woman sat down and excused Ashley to go in the bathroom to get ready while she waited with Allison. From that moment on, the girls were never alone and Ashley was waiting for Allison at the door when it was time for her to go to the theater for dress rehearsal.

Each chaperon stood beside their twin and would stick by their side until bedtime on Saturday night, after the play was over. Allison hugged her sad sister and with comforting words said, "Ashley, I know you will be with me in spirit and give me the support I will need, even from here."

"I know you will be great, Allison, almost as good I would have been." Giving her a hug, she tried hard not to cry. "Remember Mr. Brown will be filming Juliet's part, so please, just do the best you can. I'll be praying for you."

"Thanks Ashley, I can use a lot of prayer." Taking one last look at her sad sister, Allison followed Mrs. Ward out to her car.

CHAPTER 36

"Darn! How in the heck did you girls pull off a switch if those old hawks never let you out of their sight?" Dalton was completely stumped and David was no better off.

"I agree with my friend Dalton, ladies. Just how did you make a switch or did Allison actually perform the role of Juliet and fool Mr. Roy Brown into believing she was really Ashley? He'd have no way of knowing you girls switched places so he would have put Ashley Andersen on the label as the one playing Juliet."

"That's right David, I never thought of that solution." Dalton looked at the smiling twins. "Well, did my girl play Juliet or did you magically find a way to switch places?"

"That's were being close identical twins pays off and it did this time for sure." Allison recalled what had happened. "I was reading in bed when Ashley came through the door, upset and crying. When she finally was able to talk, she filled me in on the movie and the unfortunate trip to Joes that cost her the lead in Romeo and Juliet. I had never seen my sister this upset before and I realized then, Ashley's dream to become an actress was the only thing that could fulfill her life and make her completely happy. Like Ashley, I still had my dream of being a mother and raising lots of children so I knew I would have to go about it the conventional way, fall in love, get married, then have my beautiful children. Ashley had planned it out and knew if the right producer saw her acting, she could be an instant success. Life has taught us to follow our dreams and if they're meant to be, your dreams will come true. And just as we dreamed, Ashley has become a box office hit and I have a home filled with happy children. But it seemed like Ashley's dreams were about to be crushed."

"In my mind I kept trying to figure out how Allison and I could pull off a switch." Ashley remembered thinking the end of her world had come and she knew by Mr. Walker's tone ordering a council meeting with the home board immediately, that this punishment was going to be more severe than those in her past.

"Allison, they might separate us tomorrow or put me in solo detention, so there's no way we can do the bathroom swap, like in the past."

"We'll think of something Ashley, even if it means staying up all night." Allison had laid down her book when her sister walked in crying and she noticed her trembling fingers as she tried to plait her hair after sliding on the pajamas. "If we put our heads together, I know we can come up with the right solution." Feeling sorry for her repeated tries at platting, Allison got up to help her sister. "Just take a deep breath and relax, Ashley. I'll braid your hair for you."

"Allison, why did you stop braiding your hair at bedtime?" Ashley closed her eyes, happy in her heart she had such a loving sister. "You wear your hair straight now. Are you tired of sleeping in a braid?"

"I'm happy to know you can get your mind off your problems for a little while, sis, talking about our hair." Getting to the end of the pigtail, Allison wrapped a band neatly around it. "If you must know, I was getting tired telling our teacher at school which twin I was. I figure with my hair straight and yours in curls, she would know without asking. Then we just stopped talking and stared at one another for what seemed like a whole minute before we started taking off our pajamas and swapping them. Ashley smiled as she took down her long pigtail and brushed it out straight. I braided my hair in an exact copy of hers and secured it on the end. I unfastened my necklace that Grandmother Andersen gave me and placed it around Ashley's neck while she took of her drama ring and slipped it on my middle finger where she always wore it. Laughing softly, I climbed into her bed while she climbed into mine and said as she picked up my book:

"I'm glad you're feeling a little better Ashley. Just try and get some sleep while I finish this chapter." Then we giggled like young schoolgirls knowing in the morning we would be ready and no one would guess we had swapped places."

"So, you pulled it off again!" David laughed at the sneaky geniuses. "My beautiful actress played Juliet, got her screen shots to send to Hollywood and I assumed you were called eventually for an interview with a top producer."

"Not a call but a certified letter from a big producer from M.G.M Studios in Hollywood, California!" Ashley recalled the day the letter arrived was almost the same hour as Mr. Jeffrey Everhart, of Everhart and Avery law firm arrived from Ashville, North Carolina. "He explained to me and Allison that my father had left a small sum of money to us, due to his age and paying off a big mortgage, he hadn't started putting back very much money for the future, thinking he had time to start saving later, never knowing his life would be cut short, along with your mother. However, Mr. Andersen did take out a small life insurance policy which has had time to build over the thirteen years you have been here at Angel of Mercy. It is your parents wish that you, Ashley and Allison cash in the life insurance policy when you graduate high school and start your choice of careers." The lawyer peered over his black rim glasses as he spoke. "I regret it's not enough to send both of you to college, but divided and spent well, it should see you both through until you can find employment and a place to rent, perhaps together, to share in expenses." He forced a smile and added "With the small savings of $500 and the policy being $5,000, that comes to $5500 and after the lawyer's fee of $400, that leaves you a total of..."

"We can add, Mr. Everhart. That gives us $2,550 apiece and unless you were referring to one of us attending some community college, neither of us could afford to go if we had all of it!" "I must admit, I was disappointed that this man could take advantage of two orphans who had nothing but the clothes on our backs and a few personal items to our name. The least he could have done was charge us half price and write off half as charity. So, when the letter from Hollywood arrived twenty minutes later, my emotions were mixed. On one side, I was overjoyed to hear from such a wonderful studio, but on the flip side, I had to pack my bags and head out west to Hollywood or miss out on this great opportunity. My emotions must have been showing on my face, because Allison started shaking me with excitement, wanting to know what it said. So, I began reading."

"Miss Andersen, we have seen your screen test and are very impressed. Not only with your gorgeous young face and very mature body, but your acting ability seems to flow naturally. You were outstanding in the balcony scene and the tears when you awoke and found that Romeo had taken his own life, were genuine and completely realistic. If you are seriously interested in acting for film, we are very interested and we require no art school education from such a gifted, young lady. There is a small part in our next film we think will be perfect for you, but we need you to fly out to Hollywood by the first of next week or the part will be handed out to our second choice. We request an answer through overnight certified mail. The movie, which has already begun filming, is a major motion picture staring a well- known actor and actress and you will have the role as their high school daughter. We hope you understand the urgent need for an immediate response. Harvey Harrison." I folded the letter and fell in the nearest chair, feeling overwhelmed and somewhat depressed, but Allison was full of excitement and optimism as she cheerfully said:

"Things will work out Ashley! This is what you've always wanted and now you have the chance to do the one thing you are great at!"

"Yes, I know Allison, but I wasn't prepared for such an Immediate request! How can I possibly go now? I had expected to find a job and make enough money to add to my half of the inheritance! There just isn't enough money to buy the clothes I need, a set of luggage, personal items, cosmetics and toiletries! Then there is taking a bus to the big city to catch my airplane, which is another big expense. After I arrive in Hollywood, I have to find a small apartment, if there is one available, and the prices in California are so much more than they are here in N.C." Ashley dropped her head back against the chair. "Now I must spend some of the money for a certified letter and when I arrive at the Los Angelis Airport, there's another fee for transportation to the address on this letter! It is impossible! I'll just have to decline and try to explain the reason."

"You will do no such thing Ashley Andersen!" Allison pulled her sister up from her chair. "You are going to the post office right this minute and informed Harvey Harrison you gratefully except and will be in Hollywood sometime Monday morning!"

"Allison, I would like nothing more, but it can never be done!" Ashley tried to put on a good front. "I'm sure I will get another chance, after I have the money."

"Movie producers can be hard-headed if they are refused by some unknown, and hoping for another chance is tricky, dear sister." Slipping on a light sweater and handing Ashley's hers, she started for the door. "Now, stop worrying about the money. Five thousand dollars will take care of everything you need! The extra fifty you have can buy your food until you get paid."

"Oh, no Allison, I cannot take your half, it isn't fair!" Ashley felt tears fill her blue eyes. "I know how much you love me. I also know you would do anything for me, if it meant making me happy. You have proved it over and over, by taking my place every time I got grounded. You missed out on so many things because of my foolish mistakes." Ashley looped her arms around her twin in a sisterly hug. "Just the offer is most precious to me, but I'll think of another way. I can never take your inheritance."

"You can and you will! I'll be fine right here in Antler Knob, Ashley. You'll always have a home to return to. I've already had several good, job offers, one as the secretary for the Methodist Church when Mrs. Clark retires next week." Taking Ashley's hand, Allison headed for the post office, four blocks away. "I have already put a down payment down on a very cute apartment near the church, so I can walk to work. I managed saving two hundred dollars cleaning Doctor and Mrs. Fowler's home this past year and with my fifty from mama and daddy's savings, after the lawyer took the other four hundred, I have one hundred and eighty dollars in the bank." Allison stopped just outside the post office and looked in her sister's eyes. "Ashley, I know if it was me that needed something, you would be right there to see that I got it. You and I have always been there for each other and I know it is something that will live inside us forever."

"And it has been, after all the years that have passed and the distance between us. When I look at my reflection in the mirror, I see Allison, and feel her next to me. There is a bond between us that will never cease."

"And it has shone in every sacrifice you made for one another." David put his arm around Ashley as they walked down the street to Dalton's car. "Allison, you were so right when you told your sister she would be there for you, if it was you who needed her. I can't imagine such incredible love. Being in the spotlight like you were and trying to keep four pregnancies quiet was a true test of love."

"Just like Allison giving her inheritance to Ashley to fulfill her dream, Ashley in turn, fulfilled my girl's dream, by making sure she got the children that has made her life complete." Dalton stopped to hug Allison as he concluded "Two loving sisters with giving hearts."

"I think the hardest part came when we had to say goodbye at the Antler Knob Train Station the day I met you, Dalton." Allison remembered how they had to rush, shopping for what Ashley needed and calling the airport for airline tickets to L.A. and discovering the fastest way to Ashville was by rail. The time had arrived and suddenly reality hit home to the twins.

"I don't know when I will be able to get back for a visit, Allison!" tears began to flow down Ashley's cheeks, the thought of not seeing her sister every single day for God knew how long. "I cannot imagine being apart from you. It will be like leaving half of me behind."

"Perhaps time will ease the feeling of separation, dear sister." The train speaker cracked as a nasal voice called for passengers to get aboard. Allison grabbed her sister, and held her tight, not wanting to let her go as she whispered through her sobs. "I will miss you terribly Ashley! I almost wished we could erase the years and go back when we were safe at home with mama and daddy!"

"Even though that is impossible Allison, we can cherish all

the years we had together and hold them in our hearts!" she felt the conductor's hand on her shoulder as he solemnly spoke.

"I know goodbyes are hard, especially when you've never been apart from one another, but it won't be forever." Joey Allen, a home orphan himself, knew how close Allison and her sister Ashley were and wanted to make it easier for them. "This old train runs every day from Ashville and the airplanes make cross country travel a lot quicker. "Why, when you become that famous star, Ashley Andersen, you can afford to visit any old time, right?"

"Thanks Joey!" Ashley picked up her overnight case and slung her bag over her shoulder. "Take care of yourself Allison."

"You're the one who gets into trouble, remember? I won't be there to exchange places with you, so behave yourself and hurry back home!"

"And with one more hug, we waved goodbye, me standing in the station and Ashley, waving from the train window." Allison smiled up at Dalton. "I remember watching Ashley's train leave the station as I heard the inbound train coming down the tracks, never knowing there was a man on that train about to steal my heart."

CHAPTER 37

"Tyler, I have only ten minutes before I leave for dress rehearsal!" Robin had been trying to eat her early supper, and her younger brother kept knocking her arm, picking with Jonathan. Ignoring their sister's pleas, the two boys kept hitting one another until the twelve-year-old had enough and jerked them both up and started poking Tyler in his shoulder with her finger.

"Now, listen here Tyler, if you two don't stop this fighting at the supper table, I am going to march right inside that kitchen and fetch mama's flyswatter, and whop you on the head, understand?"

"Ow!" Tyler wiggled out of her grip. "Golly gee sis, do you have to keep poking my arm?"

"Do you have to keep spoiling my supper, you little morons!" Robin stopped talking when her mother walked inside the house with Reverend Lane. "Mama, can you tell these two boys, fighting is not allowed at the supper table!"

"Fighting?" Allison placed a hand on each boy's head. "What's this about fighting at the table?"

"Gosh mama, we weren't fighting, we were only playing, right Jon?" Tyler rubbed his sore arm.

"Sure! That's all, Mama!" Jonathan frowned at his sister. "Robins been acting uppity ever since she came home from that fancy birthday party, dressed like a princess. I think it went to her head and she thinks she can boss us around!"

"I never said I felt like a princess, you little toad!" Robin looked over at Dalton Lane, observing her closely. "Grumpy old Mr. Conner, Ellen's rich doctor father, had to bring me home and he kept going on about driving his Mercedes in our neighborhood, hoping none of his friends would see him. Well, I just took all the hateful remarks I could stomach and told the old grouch if any of his wealthy friends happen to see him passing through our poor little neighborhood, then they would have to be driving around in here too!"

"Darling, do you feel alright? It's not like you to let things upset you like this." Allison felt relieved when Clara stepped from the kitchen carrying a fresh pot of coffee. "Clara, did you happen to see the gentleman who brought Robin home from the party. I recall you telling us, someone was to bring her home.

"And, someone did, sweet girl, only it wasn't the Doctor who was supposed to bring her. He got called in the hospital for an emergency." Her big toothy smile spread over her cheerful face. "Mellie Townsend went into early labor, and three precious little babies came into this world while grouchy old Doctor Conner was forced to replace the baby doctor's home delivery." She chuckled. "I graciously thanked the rich snob and remembering his life before college, I ask him how his parents, Henry and Betsey were making out at the nursing home since they retired from hog farming. I can't recall seeing a brighter shade of red on any face before, as he backed down the sidewalk nervously and got back into that big old car and speed away."

"It certainly made my day better Clara, until these two started fighting while I was trying to eat." Robin slipped on her coat when she noticed Reverend Lane getting out his car keys. "I'm ready if you are, Reverend Lane."

"I'm ready." Dalton wanted to kiss Allison goodbye, but knew until the kids knew their intentions, he would refrain from his wants. "It will probably be a long evening, Allison. The good news is, we have the theater for the reminder of the night. The art school was there this morning and rehearsed all day. Ashley's director is setting up the stage right now and after costumes are handed out, we will start rehearsing." Dalton reached for her hand. "Billy, the Hollywood director knows good talent when he sees it Allison. He came by the church early this morning and saw the life size nativity scene you and Joseph made for the sanctuary. With Joseph's great carpentry work and your excellent painting skills, those figures can all but talk. He asked to use them for the second act, our sacred carols."

"I am impressed. I'm sure the studio designers are very talented and educated professionals." Suddenly the room started spending and Allison found herself falling. Lucky for her, Dalton quickly reached out and caught her, lifting her up in his strong arms.

"Mama! What's wrong?" Robin grew white with worry.

"Your mama is just a wee bit tired, baby girl. I think she might have overdone her day out with her sister reminiscing old times." Clara opened the door to Allison's bedroom. "I think after she has taken her medicine, which she seemed to have forgotten due to her excitement, she will start feeling better." Clara motioned for the preacher to bring her over to the bed while she turned down the covers. "Alright, Dalton, gently lay her down and hold up her head so she can take this medicine."

"You're right Clara, I simply forgot to take my pills." Allison smiled up weakly. "Being out with Dalton and Ashley with David, was so pleasant, I never once thought about being so sick. I know it may sound foolish, but I really felt good, like my old self."

"It doesn't sound foolish at all, sweet girl. Sometime a day out with the ones you love and who love you in return, is the best medicine around." Now, you just close your eyes and get some rest. I'll see that the children are entertained and go to bed on time."

"Thank you, Clara." Allison knew Dalton and Robin would be late if he didn't leave now. "Clara, may I have a quick word with Dalton before he and Robin has to go?"

"Of course, you may, Allison. Just make it fast before that strong dose of medicine kicks in and helps you fall asleep. Father Lane, like they say in show business, break a leg tonight!" Chuckling to herself, the jolly woman went to round up the other four children for a quiet game.

"Dalton darling" she held his hand lovingly. "I hope everything goes well tonight and you don't have any more dropouts from your group. You will make sure Robin remembers to button her coat and wrap up her head and put on her gloves. Sometimes she forgets to put on the scarf or gloves and if her mind is on the play, she will leave her coat flapping open."

"She's my daughter too, sweetheart. Don't worry about our little girl, I'll make certain she's wrapped up nice and warm." Dalton bent down and kissed her tired lips. "Now, young lady, close those beautiful blue eyes and get the rest you deed. Tomorrow will be a long day, filled with Christmas Eve activities and you'll need all the energy you can muster. I'll want you to cheer us on in the concert contest and our kid's will be expecting a visit from Santa Claus tomorrow night."

"I want you to be here to help me greet Santa when he comes down the chimney." Allison said, feeling drowsy.

"I would be honored, my dearest love." He smiled as he watched her drift off into a restful sleep and whispered, "To be here with you on Christmas Eve and to spend Christmas day with my family, is one Christmas Miracle come true." He kissed her forehead and slipped out the door.

CHAPTER 38

Clara had got the four youngest children interested in Rook, a favorite of the Stevens. All seem to be going well until Jonathan announced, "I have the Ravin!"

"Look dummy, you are not supposed to yell out what card you have!" Taylor squinted his eyes at her younger brother. "Besides, moron, the Rook is not a Ravin! It's a stupid crow!"

"Stupid crow?" Tyler sat up, shaking his head. "I'll have you know crows are very smart! They are almost as smart as humans!"

"Tyler, get out of here!" Taylor laughed, joined by Jonathan. "A dumb crow cannot be as intelligent as a person! You maybe, but not me!"

"Where did you learn that, Tyler? Your dumber than dumb bird book?" Jonathan fell back laughing.

"No wise guy, I heard in on the educational channel! True facts and they even had footage of a crow hugging its mate with his wing!"

"Clara, how come when Taylor, Tyler, and Jonathan fight, they don't poke the other one in the arm like Robin does?" Hannah had been silently observing the three going at one another.

"Yeah?" Tyler calmed down and waited for Clara to answer. "Robin has poked me several times when she's mad! Always on my upper shoulder! It still hurts from this afternoon!"

"Oh, it could be almost any reason why some people lash out. A bad habit or even a family trait, passed down from one generation till the next." Clara smiled brightly at their questioning faces. "Have you ever seen your mama or daddy poke someone like that if they get upset?"

"Mama's practically a saint and daddy couldn't even whip our old dog Maggie when she tore up the sofa." Tyler scratched his head while he thought. "I know I've seen somebody, a man

I think, poking someone in the upper arm as he was giving them what's what!"

"I've got it! I just saw him last Sunday going after Clarence Hill!" Jonathan sat straight up, eyes wide with excitement. "I had to excuse myself, really bad during preaching. Miss Apple, our Sunday school teacher had brought some refreshments and I had three glasses of strawberry punch. So, after wiggling around in my seat for ten minutes, mama excused me." Jonathan recalled coming from the boy's restroom and hearing arguing down the hall. "I saw Reverend Lane have Mr. Hill cornered and the preacher was letting him have it! I held my breath, hoping they wouldn't see me watching and to my relief, they didn't!"

"Jonathan, why was Dalton fussing with that man? He must have done something really bad to pull our devoted minister out of the service.!" Hannah had always called the minister by his first name, because she felt drawn to him.

"I heard him tell Clarence Hill to stay away from Allison Stevens and stop flirting with her in front of her children and his own wife, Hilda! Reverend Lane was poking him repeatedly in his shoulder, just like Robin does you, Tyler! The preacher got real mad when Clarence brushed it off saying it wasn't no crime to look at a beauty woman and admire her charming ways." The eight-year-old boy shook his head. "Reverend Lane said, the sin was not just admiring a pretty woman, it was the way you were looking at her and the thing you said! Remember Clarence? You said if you ever get lonesome, pretty girl, since your man's gone, give me a call. I know how to cheer up a pretty little thing like you."

"Ah! Come on now, preacher" Clarence gave this real sick laugh as he chugged his drooping shoulders. "I only meant I could give her a little adult company, just being around kids and all."

"Then what happened?" Taylor had got up on her knees, curious to know what happened next.

"Mrs. Hill stepped up and slapped Clarence on his face!" Jonathan chuckled as he remembered the preacher smiling and Hilda's shocked husband, staring wide-eyed at his wife, who had heard everything."

"Now that you mention it, I remember Mr. Hill coming over to mama when the congregation was going around shaking hands with one another. I couldn't exactly hear what he told her, but she looked away, embarrassed." Tyler got up off the floor to stretch his legs. "I saw Reverend Lane say something to the assistant minister and leave. Wow!"

"You know, I can remember another time Reverend Lane was angry with that mean old man that used to say things to daddy when he was sick." Taylor recalled the Sunday when the children's choir were singing for communion. "Reverend Lane said there would be a slight change in the service that day. Everyone was supposed to bring up their offering when they took the bread and wine. He had preached on leaving your offering at the altar if you had a disagreement with someone. Then go and take care of your...grievance..." Taylor looked at Clara "Clara, what does grievance, mean?"

"Grievance is like a complaint for something someone has done wrong between two or more people. The Lord does not want His children to bring Him an offering if they are mad with someone. Go make up with that person, then come back to the altar, pick up your offering and put it in the plate." Clara smiled, glad to know the children listen to the preacher's sermons. "I take it the good reverend saw this Conner's man as one who needed forgiveness by someone?"

"Well, I could hear them talking just behind the doors that come out inside the sanctuary. Reverend Lane said he knew how cruel he had spoken to Joseph Stevens before he passed away. Sometimes in front of Allison and other times in front of the children." Taylor's eyes were big as she recalled the harsh way Mr. Collings was staring at the preacher. "That mean old Mr. Collins was giving poor Dalton a 'go to hell' look, as daddy called it but the preacher didn't seem to care as he kept on poking the rude man in the shoulder." She gave Clara a shy smile when she added "I know I shouldn't have, but I was kinda hoping Dalton would hit the big brut!" Taylor giggled "But I sure was proud when our brave preacher pointed to the back door and told him to go ask his wife for forgiveness for the many times he hurt her by flirting with a dying man's wife!

Then he told Collins to get on his knees and ask God to forgive him and when he felt right with Jesus in his heart, to come back and lay his offering in the plate. He would be excepted back into the fold!"

"What did old man Collins say or do?" Tyler had heard the rude man criticize his daddy and laugh at him when he stumbled from weakness. He couldn't see the man ever praying to God.

"He narrowed his bitty eyes and said he didn't need forgiveness from his old lady and as for his being excepted back into this rotten fold, preacher man, just keep dreaming! I don't see no need in prayer! Then Reverend Lane stepped away, looking pretty sorrowful, knowing this man needing a lot of prayers and told him he would pray for his soul and truly hoped he would see the errors of his way. Without another word, the preacher walked away and left Mr. Collins staring after him, until he turned and stormed out of the church."

"I hope Dalton gave that man a lot of pokes!" Hannah said as tears filled her blue eyes. "Poor daddy! Why didn't the bad man die instead of my daddy?"

"Baby girl, sometimes the Lord gives sinners a longer time in hopes that their heart will become good." Clara gathered up the small girl. "Now, your daddy was a good man and he was ready to see heaven, so he would feel well again."

"Clara, mama is sick now! She won't be going to heaven too and leave us, will she?" Hannah laid her head on Clara's shoulder.

"I cannot know what the Lord has planned, sweet baby, but tomorrow is Christmas Eve, Bella is a perfect match for your mama. The chances are very good that we are going to have a Christmas Eve miracle tomorrow night."

"But Mama's surgery is after Christmas Clara!" Taylor was thoughtful "Don't you mean a miracle the day after Christmas?"

"Christmas Eve, the day after Christmas, who cares? As long as Mama has that miracle!"

CHAPTER 39

Tyler walked over to the mantle and glazed up at the old nativity scene with the baby missing. "I wonder if the missing baby got burned up in Mama and Aunt Ashley's house?"

"You might just get your answer this Christmas, Tyler." Clara rocked Hannah in her arms as she smiled up at the cherished old manger scene.

"I'm wondering about another mystery, right here at home!" Taylor saw she had everyone's attention. "Why does Robin poke Tyler in the shoulder just like Reverend Lane?"

"Yeah! And have you noticed, she is the only one that has black hair and green eyes…" Tyler's eyes grew round. "Like Dalton Lane! The rest of us have blonde hair and blue eyes."

"Just like your mama!" Clara sat up rubbing Hannah's head. "Which one of you look like you daddy?"

"I guess none of us got daddy's hair or brown eyes!" Jonathan looked at his sisters and brother.

"No, you didn't take after Joseph, your daddy." Clara knew telling children the truth would not come easy as she said. "If the four of you take after your mama, which one takes after your daddy?"

"Robin." Hannah sat up, eyes wide with understanding. She was the youngest, but she had felt the fatherly pull from the preacher she loved. "Clara, if Dalton is our daddy, was daddy our daddy too?"

"Yes, he was, sweet baby, in all the ways a daddy can be. He raised you and gave you more love than you can possibly imagine." Clara knew she must choose her words wisely, for the Father had put these small ones in her care. "Sometimes daddies cannot make babies, due to health problems, so his babies have to come from someone who loves him very much."

"Reverend Lane?" Taylor sat down at Clara's feet as Tyler and Jonathan followed.

"Your daddy and Dalton Lane grew up together in an

orphanage and became the very best of friends. Since your daddy always had health problems, his best friend was always there for him. When he found out he couldn't give your mama babies, he asked his friend to help him. When you grow up and can understand how babies come from heaven to loving parents, you will understand everything." Clara smiled, showing true love. "Dear children, never doubt, for one minute, that Joseph Stevens is your daddy in every way. No father out there could have loved you more than he did." She placed a hand on each child. "Now, it is time for you to show love to your other daddy. He is not here to take your daddies place but to continue to help the friend he loves so much make sure those little babies, you, my precious ones, have a daddy, to love you in the same way as his dear friend, Joseph." She looked at each child, tears in their blue eyes as she asked, "Can you love him the way he has always loved you?"

"Gee whiz, Clara, I can't just say right now!" Tyler stood up, his young eyes serious. "I gotta know how mama feels about all this. Maybe if it's alright with her, then it will make my decision a little easier."

"I'm with Tyler on this one, Clara." Taylor joined her twin brother. "How can anyone expect us to love Reverend Lane like we loved our daddy?"

"Because, my dear loving children, your daddy loved him." Allison had been listening and was glad it was Clara who had told the children about Dalton. Now, it was up to her to help them love him as their father. "Some time back, before I married your daddy, I met Dalton Lane and fell madly in love with him. The two of us was so in love, Dalton was just about to ask me to marry him."

"If you loved him that much, Mama, why didn't you marry Dalton instead of Daddy?" Taylor couldn't understand two people that much in love and not getting married.

"I never knew the reason until recently, darling." Like Clara, Allison knew her words must be chosen wisely for young children to understand. "When Joseph, your daddy came in town to visit Dalton, I started to see a change in the man I had fallen in love with. He kept his distance while pushing

Joseph in my arms. I never knew why he seem so willing to be the minister who married me and Joseph and was always there to celebrate an anniversary or the birth of our babies."

"What made Reverend Lane change, mama. Why did he stop loving you?" Tyler felt proud that his beautiful mother would share all her secret memories with them.

"Child, Dalton Lane never stopped loving your mama. That is why he never got married. She was the only woman he knew he could ever love." Clara nodded when Allison gave her a silent thank you. "When your daddy showed up at Dalton's house, he was about a low as a man could get. Crying his heart out to the only one he knew he could depend on. Now, your daddy had no ideal Dalton was in love with Allison, so he kept going on how much he loved this girl named Ali, his nickname for Allison. Your daddy met her when she still lived at the orphanage. Joseph had come to Antler Knob to build new shelves for the town library and your mama, along with other home girls had the job of taking the books off the old shelves and storing them in order. Joseph was completely smitten with your mama, but she only considered him a good friend. He said if he could find her and marry her, it would make him the happiest man alive and he would love her as long as he lived."

"Up until that statement, Dalton was about to tell his friend about his love for me and he would be asking for my hand in marriage. When Dalton was learning to be a minister, a chaplain from the Air Force, where you daddy tried to join, right out of high school, but got turned down, told Dalton how sick your daddy was and wouldn't have long to live." Allison needed the children to understand what an outstanding man Dalton Lane was, so she continued. "Dalton said, all he could keep hearing from his friend was, happiest man alive and love her as long as he lived."

"Don't you see babies, Dalton Lane gave up his own happiness so his very best friend could have true happiness, what few years he had left." Clara noticed the tears swelling in the children's eyes and their hands clutching on to each other. "I know you need time, sweet ones, to let everything set in, but don't wait too long. How difficult would it be to love the man who gave you life so you could know and love your daddy. The man who gave up his love so your daddy could love. He truly has a giving heart!"

"He really does, Clara!" Robin stood at the door smiling. "I, for one, will proudly call Dalton Lane daddy! Tomorrow is Christmas Eve. Let us all give this man who helped bring us into this world the best present we can! Tell him we love him and want him to be our daddy now and make mama the happiest girl alive!" Robin held out her arms to her brothers and sisters and they ran over laughing and crying. "You'll find out, it easy to love someone who already loves each one of us so very much!"

"I know!" Hannah said loudly "I have loved him for ever and ever!"

Allison and Clara joined in the group hug as the happy group laughed with joy.

CHAPTER 40

The practice had gone very well and at breakfast on Christmas Eve, Robin excitedly filled in her family.

"I felt like a real Hollywood entertainer! The set was elaborate, right out of an M.G.M. musical and the costumes just as wonderful!" She tried to take small bites so she could speak. "Ronnie and daddy said I did great on my solo, even though I felt I could have been better. The first half went super good and Mr. Billy said we would have artificial snow falling tomorrow on the set. It was too messy for dress rehearsal and would need cleaning up before our performance tonight."

"How did the second half go, Robin?" Allison wondered how the church nativity worked out on such a big stage.

"The set was perfect mama! The true-to-life wood characters stand out even more beautifully under the stage lights and spots Billy brought from the Hollywood studio. Aunt Ashley was there to help the famous dance instructor show us some really cool steps in the first half. Because the songs in the second half are sacred, we stand virtually still and if we lose anymore singers from church, it won't sound as full as Ronnie would like." Robin looked thoughtful, remembering the last song. "Daddy does the solo so very beautiful in O Holy Night, but when the choir comes in it sounds too weak. I think the final number needs to be the most spectacular, especially after the first half is as good as anything the art school has ever none, if not better!"

"Well then, Miss Robin, I think I may be able to help out with that last beautiful song, very appropriate for this Holy night too." Clara started collecting the dirty dishes as she chuckled remembering her young friend singing with the group. "How did Bella do with her solo last night, child?"

"Bella sounded like an angel, Clara!" Robin recalled her clear high voice. "If we had a few more Bella's singing in the last half, we would be sure to win, hands down!"

"Then I just happen to know some very angelic sounding ladies and gentlemen who have lived and worked right here in Antler Knob!" Clara beamed "Like the fine young gentleman who filled in for me last evening, playing the piano."

"Simon?" Robin recalled the choir director worrying when Clara never showed up to play as promised and this young man showing up saying he would be filling in for Clara, just for dress rehearsal. "He said Clara had a last-minute important job to perform and she would be able to play for the program, which is today."

"That's right baby girl, when Clara gets an assignment from her loving boss, she happily performs." Clara walked to the kitchen humming Silent Night.

The Antler Knob Theater had never been so packed as it was this Christmas Eve and television stations from all the networks had shown up and been placed up in the small top balcony. The wires and cameras would be kept away from the paying audience. Front row seating had been arranged for Allison and her four children, along with David. The M.C. stepped out on the stage to a loud round of clapping, glad the show would soon start.

"Good evening, ladies and gentlemen, welcome to the Antler Knob Theater. A very special welcome to all the children and young people as well. We welcome tonight, three judges who have been chosen because of their expertise in the fine arts. Before I introduce these outstanding people, I will go over our rules for competing in the Christmas Eve Concert Contest and a few new rules relating to the judges. First, those who enter this contest must be connected to our small town, either by work, school, or have or still do call Antler Knob their home. Tonight, we have two groups competing for the big prize. They will share the stage, Group one, the Antler Knob School of the Arts, will be performing on the left side of the stage and group two, The Methodist Church will entertain us on the right side. Each group will have one hour to perform, split in two halves. Group one will do their first thirty-minute show, followed by group two's show. There will be a brief intermission for an important announcement and a chance to go to the restrooms, then Group one will have their last thirty minutes show, followed by group two." The master of ceremonies waved at both curtains and smiled as he announced, "We would like to thank the director from the M.G.M. studios in California for loaning us the double curtains and divider in the center of the stage, this way neither group knows what the other has behind their curtain." He turned and motioned to those waiting to be called.

"Now, it gives me great pleasure to introduce our judges for this year's contest. The first judge I will introduce should be familiar with those who have attended this contest before. A warm welcome to Harvey Parsons, a talent agent from New York City." Those watching gave him a respectful but short applause. "Our next judge has directed many box office movies! From the M.G.M. studios in Hollywood, please welcome "Billy!" The applause was somewhat louder and lasted longer than the first judge. "Now, it gives me great pleasure to introduce a very beautiful, very talented and most important home-grown girl from right here in Antler Knob, actress, Miss Melinda Star!" This time the crowd rose to their feet and the loud clapping seemed to last a good minute before settling down when the three judges took their seat down front at a small table supplied with a pen and tablet for each judge.

"Now, judges, this will be the first year in having three people to choose the best and most creative group as the winner. The winner must be voted on with complete agreement from all three judges. Before, we had only the one judge, but since the winnings have increased the secret Santa feels three judges, making the same decision is only fair and just. The pad is for you to keep your points on for creativity, performance, costume and set design. Good luck and may the best group win! Now, let the show begin with Group one's theme: 'Rock around the Christmas Tree.'"

The curtain opened to a giant artificial silver Christmas tree with sparkling color lights flashing overhead. Dancers came on stage, dressed like gift wrapped presents and went into a fast version of O Christmas Tree and changing words about presents under the tree. A couple came out and hung some mistletoe, acted shy then kissed as a group of couples appeared dressed like the 60's but all Christmas colors as they sang and danced to Rocking around the Christmas Tree.

The group went on for thirty minutes singing many popular Christmas hits, all with the sound of rock and the schools dancers fell into several dances to make their first half, exciting. Their bow brought a lot of applause before settling down for the M.C. to announce the church group.

"That's what you might call, a little bit of Christmas and a whole lot of rock and roll! Now, group two brings you the warm and whimsical 'I'll Be Home for Christmas' theme!"

The curtain opened up to Bella, standing at a train depot, looking down the track for her inbound train as she started singing: "I'll Be Home for Christmas". As she sang, the train stopped and she got abroad and continued to sing next to a window as the train appeared to be moving along a snow-covered country side. Arriving to where the sign read: Antler Knob, Bella went inside only to have the depot wall move away and reveal the small town of Antler Knob. Every streetlight was a glow and decorated with holly and berries. The shops seem to come alive with Christmas displays and people walking up and down the street singing "It's Beginning to Look a Lot Like Christmas" Bella is greeted by a horse and sleigh and a handsome driver, Dalton Lane, climbs down and helps the lady up as a group of young people jump out from the back and start singing "Sleigh Ride". A country road scene drops down and the horse moves on a moving slow-moving treadmill.

Bella is helped off the sleighed and the driver takes the horse off the scene as the last scene makes way to inside a big living room, where a live Christmas tree is being decorated by the cast as they sing "Chestnuts roasting on an Open fire" As they light up the big tree, someone pushes back a big curtain to revile the snow falling out side and they stepped out to "Winter Wonderland" As the entire cast gather around the big tree, they gazed out at the audience and sang "Have Yourself a Merry Little Christmas". They came forward and bowed to a thundering applause, knowing their first half was a spasming success.

"We hope you have enjoyed the first half of our concert contest tonight and all I can say is, I'm glad I am not one of the judges. This will not be easy to find three people in complete agreement to which one of these wonderful performances is the best" he smiled down at the studio director. "Now, my friends, the announcement I said would be coming. Some might ask why this man goes by his first name only, but he is so well known in Hollywood everyone simply knows him as, Billy!"

"It is a great privilege to be here tonight working alongside of my dear friend and great actress, Melinda Star. If you grew up here in Antler Knob, especially those who lived at Angel of Mercy Orphanage, you will best remember her by the name, Ashley Andersen. Ashley is not only a great actress but a very loving giving person and there's no one she knows or loves any better than her twin sister, Allison Andersen Stevens. The reason we are here instead of Hollywood finishing our latest film is because the loving sister dropped everything when she found out her sister was very sick and needed a kidney transplant. Thanks to a loving God and another secret Santa who is the perfect match for Allison, she has a fighting chance to live. Right before the close of the program, Reverend Dalton Lane will ask a favor from each person here this night. I hope that you receive his message and respond in a positive way." Billy looked down at Ashley and winked, "At the close of the show, Melina Star will have a very important announcement which will bring a smile to the good citizens of North Carolina. Now, on with the show!"

CHAPTER 41

The School of the Arts gave a small musical version of "The Christmas Carol" and the audience loved it as they took their final stage bow. Now, Ronnie's upbeat mood from their first big performance seemed to dim by the loud clapping. He looked over his small group, dressed in their choir robes and the single, non-moving nativity scene and tried to put on a cheerful face. Clara practically danced out, smiling like the Cheshire cat from "Alice in Wonderland."

"Now, don't you go fretting, Ronnie. That little show they just put on will look pale compared to the heavenly program we're going to bless those people with. I would go as far as to say, this is a sure way to put every man, woman and child into the real Christmas spirit!"

"I agree with Clara, Ronnie! We may be few, but we have more at stake here and we will make them feel Christmas!" Dalton smiled broadly, knowing Billy had several amazing effects to bring their carols to life. "Just direct like you do at church, my friend, from your heart. Some of our group might not be here, but God has never left us. Just remember that and rejoice. Weather we win or lose this contest Ronnie, we still win by bringing the true meaning of Christmas, not just to our town, but to those watching on national television."

"Oh, yes! We are being televised around the world!" the director swallowed when he heard them being announced. "This is it people! Just do your best, that's all I ask." Then the curtain went up and everything grew quiet as Clara started playing "Silent Night" and once again, Bella lifted up her angelic voice as the choir hummed behind her. An enormous star hung down over the stable where the realistic figures looked down on the baby in the manger. The spotlight fell gently over Mary as the ladies began to sing "Away in a Manger". The light then fell very dim on shepherds, over to one side of the stage as the choir began singing "Angels We Have Heard on High" then, when the bright and beautiful angel appeared above them, the audience could have sworn he was real. Then there were several angels floating around the male angel as the choir sang "Hark the Herald Angels Sing" Returning to the stable, the three wise men had been brought in, along with their camels as the choir sang "We Three Kings" then as Clara played softly, Dalton stepped forward with his message.

"I am not here to give a sermon but to ask for prayer. The woman I fell in love with over fifteen years ago has a rare blood disorder that has infected her kidneys and she will die without an operation. My friend Joseph, who died a few years back, and myself fathered five beautiful children with Allison. My oldest, Robin, is on stage with me tonight and has gifted you with her beautiful voice, by singing a song she wrote for this night. My other adorable children are sitting out front with their mama and my dearest love. Allison will be going into surgery the day after Christmas because, even though she needs that kidney right now, her children's happiness has always come first.

"Tonight, Christmas Eve, is a night of miracles. I've been reminded about that from two loving women I know has a connection to Heaven. The beautiful artwork surrounding us was a gift given to our church by Allison and Joseph Stevens. His carpentry magic made them began and my girl put life into each face with her paint brushes. I'm asking you to pray silently for her complete healing and that Christmas Eve miracle when we close our program with "O Holy Night".

There was a Christmas Miracle that special night as Dalton Lane began singing and every eye was closed in silent prayer as they listened. But when the choir came in singing "fall on your knees, oh hear the angel voices" suddenly the stage became alive with angelic voices and brought tears to everyone listening as well as the church choir members. Clara's friends had arrived.

"My friends, this has been one unusual night and I can feel a Christmas spirit I haven't felt since I was five years old, still at home with my parents. Excited about the coming of Christmas! I believe we are going to get that miracle Allison, maybe right here!" Ashley smiled down at her sister, tears lacing both their eyes. "I want to first give some more good news! The winner of tonight's contest is, the Methodist

Church! The other winner tonight is the Angel of Mercy Orphanage as well as every home for children in our state. The generous response from my broadcast has brought in so far, one hundred million dollars and contributions are still pouring in. From my heart, I thank you for saving my home and the home for many more orphans."

Allison was clapping when she felt something happening inside her and she didn't need a doctor to tell her what had just happened. She knew and as her eyes met Dalton, he guessed as well. The church group had been called on stage to receive their cash prize when Allison met Dalton on the stage, where he lifted her up, twirling her around! Ashley grabbed David's hand when he said,

"The great physician has healed her!"

Robin raced over as the other four children ran on the stage, hugging their mama and daddy. Christmas Eve had come. Clara and Bella knew their work here was none as they smiled lovingly at the love surrounding Allison and Ashley Andersen. There would be three more Christmas miracles waiting for the happy group when they returned home. Under the big, beautiful tree would be three gifts, the first miracle, a box for Allison, a box for Ashley and a gift made by Robin, for her daddy, which now had five names engraved. To our loving daddy! We love you! Robin, Tyler, Taylor, Jonathan, and Hannah! The twin sisters will once again get to see their parent's faces. Inside their boxes are framed portraits of Allison and Ashley, at five-years-old, with their mama and daddy.

The second miracle gift is over the fireplace mantle. The Painting of the Stevens family has one more member, the children's other daddy. Dalton is standing beside Allison with his arm around her while the children smiled down lovingly on Joseph, happy and with a glow around his face.

And waiting for the Andersen twins, something they had believed to be long gone. In an old, worn, yellowed tissue, scorched slightly around the edges, and lying on the mantle with the nativity scene, was the tiny baby boy! Yes, Christmas Eve had come and it truly was a night of miracles and many giving hearts!